T0147627

THE STOCKTON SAGA

DAWN OF THE GUNFIGHTER

STEVEN DOUGLAS GLOVER

IUNIVERSE, INC.
NEW YORK   BLOOMINGTON

The Stockton Saga
Dawn Of The Gunfighter

This is a work of fiction. All of the characters, names, incidents, organizations, and dialogue in this novel are either the products of the author's imagination or are used fictitiously.

iUniverse books may be ordered through booksellers or by contacting:

iUniverse
1663 Liberty Drive
Bloomington, IN 47403
www.iuniverse.com
1-800-Authors (1-800-288-4677)

Because of the dynamic nature of the Internet, any Web addresses or links contained in this book may have changed since publication and may no longer be valid. The views expressed in this work are solely those of the author and do not necessarily reflect the views of the publisher, and the publisher hereby disclaims any responsibility for them.

ISBN: 978-1-4401-8966-1 (sc)
ISBN: 978-1-4401-8967-8 (ebk)

Printed in the United States of America

iUniverse rev. date: 11/17/2009

Contents

PREFACE

The Stockton Saga began as a short story for a friend. Her enthusiasm for the account of a United States Marshal of the Old West over a century ago encouraged me to continue the saga. When other friends read the adventures, their requests led to longer and more detailed stories.

Thus, Cole Stockton became my companion as my psyche raced through Texas, New Mexico Territory, the Colorado Territory, and various other locales during the latter half of the 19th century. In 2006, I published a trilogy of Old West Christmas stories entitled <u>A Shiny Christmas Star: An Old West Christmas Trilogy</u>, designed initially as a gift to friends. Meet the author events and book signings in Central Texas, and internet access, gave rise to a larger audience. The message continued—write a novel with Cole Stockton as the central character. While each Stockton story stood on its own, the settings of the stories were similar and many characters appeared repeatedly. Thus, this book was conceived and grew to its present state.

My intent is to portray the Old West as it actually was, lending authenticity to the tales. As historical fiction, most of the characters are purely fictional. When persons of historical significance are present, their character and the locale was researched. When I speak of a certain weapon, pistol or rifle, I believe that it was indeed available at that time.

In all cases, my stories are purely fictional. I build character names within the recesses my mind—hoping that the name matches the character. Any similarity to an actual person is purely coincidental.

My stories are written for enjoyment only and are not intended to be historically accurate by date, incident, or actual person.

Immense gratitude is given to Gay Lynn Auld whose time and effort reviewing and editing the manuscript provided immeasurable assistance. Her suggestions for expansion and rewrite proved invaluable to the final product.

This book would not have been published without the moral support of my wife, Linda Glover. Very special thanks also to my dedicated fans—Verna Glover, Monti Eastin, Mary Hughes, Lois Weller, Helen Werner, and Jean West, who each urged me to publish a second book.

Steven Douglas Glover
Round Rock, Texas
July 2009

"The Stockton Saga: Dawn of the Gunfighter"

Dedicated to the memory of

Robert Allen Glover

1946 – 2007

and

Louis L'Amour

1908 – 1988

CHAPTER ONE

Legacy

Was it just a turn of events that destined me to become the man that I am, or was I destined by some other power of fate? I thought back to earlier years and wondered about that. In any case, it happened: I became a noted gunfighter and, eventually, a United States Marshal. For now, perhaps I should start at the beginning, as my parents related it to me and as I experienced it.

My father, Flint Stockton, told me that his family was of Anglo-Saxon descent, and that the first of the family arrived in America sometime in the late 1700's. All of them, it seems had an adventurous nature, their hearts kindled with an internal fire that led them to seek their fortunes with a westward trek.

They desired their own land to cultivate and to raise stock on, and it was evident from all that was told to me. Of those relatives, I know very little, but there were indications of Indian misfortunes, early deaths driven by disease, and just out and out murder. This early American country was a dangerous place to raise a family.

My father sometimes spoke of his own immediate family. He was born in the mountains of West Virginia sometime around the middle of 1811 or 1812. His father, Colter Stockton, was born somewhere in eastern Virginia around 1786.

It was said that Colter Stockton stood close to Andrew Jackson at New Orleans when the American ragtag army repelled the crack British Regiments sent against them.

As my father told it, *Ole Hickory* looked deep into Colter's eyes and remarked, "You got the look of adventure in your eyes, Son. That's good! America needs men like you—forever looking forward with destiny in your mind and courage in your heart. I challenge you to that task! After this war is over, go westward and follow your destiny."

And thus, Grandfather Colter Stockton moved forward in his quest for good land and a good home. He took Davy Crockett's advice and moved westward to Tennessee. Eventually, the eastern parts of Tennessee, it seemed, filled just too full of people for Colter. He sort've itched for a land where a man had no neighbors for at least forty miles. So, he packed up his family and moved again—this time to the western most regions of Tennessee.

My father, Flint Stockton, grew up being an adventurous sort in his teens, and hearing of opportunity in the West, he took it upon himself to visit Tejas, later called Texas. It was about 1828 when he left his family in Tennessee and started out on his own. He was merely a boy of seventeen, but he was determined to make his mark in the world. He made his way to the settlement of Nacogdoches where he found work with a gunsmith. He learned to repair guns and make ammunitions for various caliber pistols, muskets, and rifles, of the time. Father also became an expert marksman with each weapon, searching out an older marksman for a teacher with each gun.

Flint loved being on his own and loved Texas. He felt that he would eventually settle and make a home for himself, marry a wife, and start a family here in this land, Tejas.

Inevitably, troubles brewed between the independent thinking Texas colonies and the commanding essence of Mexico and finally, in 1836, the hostilities came to a head. Texas declared itself independent from Mexico, and the President of Mexico, one General Antonio Lopez de Santa Anna, marched upon the rebels to meet them at the city of San Antonio de Bexar. Thus, history recorded that 118 *Texians* from Tennessee, Arkansas, Virginia, Alabama, Louisiana, Kentucky, and other points east stood in defiance of Santa Anna. Today, they are now known as Texans who fell at The Alamo.

While the Mexican Army besieged The Alamo, Flint Stockton answered the call for independence and joined a Texas Volunteer Cavalry Company being formed by Captain Jasper Rollins. Rollins had been a frontier scout and general roughneck around and about Texas, especially within the subject of law and order. Since his arrival in Texas, it was rumored that he personally dispatched at least five unsavory characters within various communities before so delegated and authorized.

Jasper was an adamant leader. He stressed tactics against the Mexican Cavalry and demanded close perfection in his drills. His main thought was that his cavalry company would break the Mexican lines allowing victory to the Texas army. He worked his men toward that goal. On April 21, 1836, they met that challenge as part of Colonel Mirabeau B. Lamar's Volunteer Cavalry Corps.

Captain Rollins' cavalrymen stormed toward Mexican defenses on the extreme right of Sam Houston's Army at The Plain at San Jacinto. They drew immediate fire from the defending Mexican Army as Texas infantry regiments rushed forward, buying the infantry precious time to reach the defenses.

The cavalry charge thundered over the Mexican emplacements and decimated their left flank. Then, the cavalry thrust inward toward the middle defenses. Simultaneously, Texas infantry had just reached the barricades and were in process of overtaking the Mexican regulars with sheer determination fired continuously by shouts of *Remember the Alamo!* and *Remember Goliad!*

In only about twenty minutes the Mexican Army threw up their arms and surrendered. A cursory check found Santa Anna had somehow escaped into the surrounding wilderness as the battle ensued. Frantic calls went up, "Find that son of a bitch, Santa Anna, and bring him back here to *justice.*"

Father moved his horse alongside Jasper Rollins and together, they searched the outskirts of the battlefield, ever vigilant, to cut off any possible escape of *El Presidente, Santa Anna.* The rest of the Texas Cavalry joined in until daylight, when the search was further expanded for Santa Anna.

Finally, a shout went up! Santa Anna had been found. He had disguised himself as a lowly soldier, a private. But, when brought to the prisoner holding area, he was addressed as *El Presidente* by other Mexican prisoners as they spotted him and stood to attention. Santa Anna was summarily brought to a place, under a sprawling oak tree where General Sam Houston lay wounded, his ankle shattered by a musket ball. My father and Jasper Rollins moved to join the group of men that surrounded the wounded Houston and beleaguered Santa Anna.

Father told me, a first-hand account, about a great deal of animosity toward Santa Anna. Many Texans wanted to hang him right there on the spot. And, another faction wanted to cut his throat and have him bleed out his life before them on the ground. There were others that would have instantly shot him had it not been for General Sam.

It seems that General Sam Houston was a thinking man, and he summarily thought only of *Texas* at that time. He convinced the others that they should hold Santa Anna until *El Presidente* signed documents that gave Texas freedom from Mexico. And to this end, also, Houston had Santa Anna write orders to his generals, commanding all Mexican armies to move south of the Rio Grande and to never return to the land now called Texas.

For a while after that, Jasper and father kind've stayed close around General Sam, until he could be transported to civilization and a doctor's care. They had become quite good friends by this time, a friendship forged in battle. They talked often of various enterprises that each individually could begin within the new Republic of Texas.

For the immediate moment, though, they seemed destined to safeguard Santa Anna from those who would kill him anyway, regardless of what General Sam wanted. And so, my father and Jasper formed a bond that would guide my own ways years later.

Once Texas was deemed safe from any further invading army, and Santa Anna returned to Mexico, my father and Jasper parted company. Each followed his own destiny. Father heard about massacring Indian raids along the northern frontier and went to join assembling forces forming for settlement defense. For the next few years, my father spent time on the frontier, learning all he could about Indian warfare, tracking, and hunting. He became somewhat expert in wilderness life and survival from the elements.

I surmise that in the early summer of five years hence, my father, Flint Stockton, rode proudly on his way toward West Texas. He had served gallantly with the Texas cavalry against the Mexican army, and lived to see the new freedom thriving within every Texas heart. Enthralled with Texas, he went to great lengths to learn all he could about the territory along the Texas frontier.

Now, it was time. My father wanted to build a life for himself. He had heard from trail scouts and various travelers that the West Texas plains held vast numbers of wild horses and wild cattle for capture. He intended to catch some of those animals and start himself the makings of a ranch.

CHAPTER TWO

Flint

On the way northward, close to a Brazos River crossing, Flint Stockton came across a wagon train of settlers traveling westward that had camped for the evening. Father could smell the delicious aroma of stew, roasting meat, coffee boiling, and most of all, the unmistakable aroma of fresh bread.

Flint dearly loved to bite into and savor warm bread. His own mother baked quite often and Flint would practically beg her to let him sample the wares before supper. She was a good woman, relenting to his wishes. She once jokingly told him, "Flint, you'll eventually marry a woman just because she can make a good loaf of fresh bread." She didn't know then just how true that was to become.

He urged his dark chestnut horse toward the flickering campfires and called out to "Hallo the camp." He was hailed back to "Enter and be welcome." Flint rode through the circle of wagons and into the firelight, where he dismounted his lanky six-foot frame and stood for all to see.

If ever there was a dashing plains figure, it was Flint. He wore a buckskin shirt open at the collar with a flowing yellow and blue neckerchief. Dark homespun trousers were tucked into worn boots with large rowled silver Mexican-style spurs.

A wide brimmed, low-crown brown hat was pulled down slightly in front to shield his eyes from the westward sun. He had sandy colored hair with his face and hands tanned by the elements.

Most noticeable about him was the manner in which he wore the two Paterson five-shot Colt revolving pistols around his slim waist. They rested somewhat low, close to hand. Flint also carried a large Bowie knife in a sheath behind his belt. A .69 caliber Plains rifle rested easy in his left hand.

All of the men in the wagon train carried flintlock pistols, muskets, or single shot shotguns for protection. They had heard tell of, but had never seen a revolving pistol yet, so they were all quite taken with Flint's pair of Paterson Colts.

He passed one around the group of men to let them examine it while he demonstrated the loading and operation with his second revolver. Duly impressed, one man in particular spoke up, "You look like you've ridden a fair piece. I'll bet that you could use a good meal and some rest."

"That I could, Sir."

"It would please me and my family if you would partake of supper with us. You may bed down close to our two wagons for the night if you wish."

"That would suit me fine, Sir."

"A-w-w-w, don't call me Sir. My name is Robert McKenna. This is my wife Elsa and our sons Grady, Sean, and Justin. Last, but not least, these are our daughters: Mary Elizabeth and Johanna Marie."

Flint gallantly swept off his wide brimmed hat in the manner of a cavalier and bowed slightly. When he looked up, his eyes met and held for an instant with those of Johanna. She was silently but gaily amused with him.

At about five foot seven, with auburn colored hair, Johanna was slender but fully a woman and curvaceous. She had graceful movements, and her hazel eyes shined with admiration, as well as just a hint of fun and mischief. They smiled at each other, a silent message passing between them with their eyes. That message became a bond to last an eternity.

Flint Stockton and the McKenna family sat around the campfire eating and talking. The warm fresh bread had drawn Flint in and he remarked so to Mrs. McKenna.

"Oh, no, Mr. Stockton, I didn't make the bread. Johanna did. She loves to bake, and she is also an excellent cook of other fare as well. Some day she, like her sister Mary Elizabeth, will make a fine wife for a good man."

Later that night as the fires died low and the cry of the coyote echoed across the prairie, Flint Stockton thought of this young woman Johanna. She was pretty, and she could cook. There was something in her eyes, something that kindled the fires of Flint Stockton's soul. He slept with these thoughts and by early morning, he knew what it was. He was in love.

Another day brought more travel for the wagon train. "Since you are headed westward," Flint announced, "I've decided to ride along with you until we reach my turning North point. After all, this is Comanche Territory and the more men that can handle firearms, the better off we'll be."

Mrs. McKenna smiled and thought, "Besides, you could get to know Johanna a bit more as we ride along."

Wagon train travel on the frontier was slow, making only about thirteen to fifteen miles a day. Flint made himself useful by riding ahead of the wagons with the scouts. He took in the landscape as he rode, his eyes constantly sweeping the horizon, watching for dangers as well as landmarks that would signal his departure point from the wagon train.

On occasion, Flint would take time to ride alongside the McKenna wagons and talk with Johanna about his plans for land and stock of his own. She spoke her thoughts of a comfortable home and family. They were drawing closer together in their thoughts. Little did they realize that they were being watched by a knowing Elsa McKenna.

Flint was well into three weeks of travel with the wagons when a band of Comanche appeared on the horizon and slowly paralleled them. Conventional wisdom at the time held that it was suicide for any Indian band to attack a well-armed wagon train. Primarily, warring Indians would track it and wait for small groups or single wagons to fall behind the main body, then they would attack.

All wagon train eyes were alert to their constant companions. No one dared to venture out of the main wagon group. When a wagon started to fall behind, several men would rush to it and give assistance to hurry it. The stock was kept close in so that the animals could be run into the center of the wagons should any trouble occur. Hour after hour, day after day, they moved without incident, but the stress of the situation was getting on people's nerves. Women fretted; men got sharp with each other.

The wagon people talked about the constant threat in small groups almost nightly until, finally, a wagon train meeting was held one night. It was nearing time for some of the wagons to turn off in southerly or northerly directions. What could they do? They couldn't just stop; they had to keep moving toward a water supply for one. No one wanted to leave the safety of the main wagon train.

Flint stood quietly in the background and observed the discussion. These people were scared. They didn't know what to do. The most immediate question posed by most of the group was "What do those heathens want?" and that was followed by a chilling speculation that "They want guns, munitions, stock, and scalps."

Intense concerns were voiced and argued back and forth as to the proper action to take until, it was finally decided that a committee of three men should ride out toward the Comanche and just ask them what they wanted.

Flint Stockton sighed silently to himself. He held the most awesome firepower. He knew that he would have to be one of those that rode out to meet with the Comanche. He stepped forward and offered his solution.

The wagon people having learned of Flint's service in the Texas War for Independence as well as his Indian fighting experience along the frontier felt relieved when he stepped forward.

"I believe that I should ride up there with two other men of stout mind and steady nerves who are armed. We will ask those Comanche just what it is they have been following us for, and then we will bargain with them to resolve it. The rest of you will stay in the wagons, encircled. A contingent of armed men should be ready to cover us in the event that we must make a hasty retreat back to the wagons."

The wagon council agreed. Two others, George Corney and Michael Flanagan, also volunteered. The three men would ride out with the first appearance of the Comanche the next morning.

Close to dawn the next morning when the Comanche once again appeared on the horizon, Flint, George Corney, and Michael Flanagan mounted and rode slowly toward the shadowy figures, right arm outstretched in a sign of friendship.

As they neared the warriors, Flint took notice of their arms. Many of the Comanche warriors held flintlock rifles, but they also carried a bow and quiver of arrows as well as their war clubs, lances, and knives. The Comanche quite noted for their horsemanship, rode magnificently trained ponies.

In previous years, Flint had learned some sign language from friends who also roamed the plains. He now used his limited sign vocabulary to ask the Comanche of their intent.

The Comanche leader signaled back that these wagons were traveling across their lands. They wanted restitution as the "loud and boisterous wagon train was scaring off the game." They wanted horses, they wanted cattle, they wanted mules, and they wanted guns, lead, and powder.

Flint signaled back, "This is a poor wagon train. We can share some, but not all that the great Comanche wants. Then the leader of the band introduced the ultimatum: The white wagon people would give the Comanche what they wanted within two suns, or they would take everything.

This meant only one thing to Flint. The Comanche were expecting others to join them, and evidently a large enough party to swarm all over the twenty-five wagons, killing everyone, and taking what they wanted.

Another thought hit Flint's mind. They also could be waiting for another group---Comancheros.

The Comanchero, ruthless scavengers, came mostly from Mexico and raided farms, ranches, and lone riders. They killed and tortured their victims, or beat them and made them slaves to sell to the Comanche. The Comanchero traded in firearms, whiskey, blankets, knives, ammunitions, cattle, horses, and just about anything of value.

Flint considered this last thought. A well armed, combined party of Comanche and Comanchero could take this wagon train within minutes. He turned to the Comanche leader and said, "We will give two cows and two horses, that is all. You will take these gifts and be gone. Should you refuse, there will be NO gifts. Should you decide to attack, the Comanche will fall before my guns like blades of grass in the great wind that destroys everything in its path. I am Great Warrior from the South and I have fought many of the Mexicanos and defeated them. My medicine is strong."

With that last gesture, Flint's right hand flashed to his revolver and he fired five shots into the air in succession.

The Comanche had never seen a revolver before and the firing of many bullets from the gun at one time excited them. Ponies shied, some bucked, and as the warriors reined them in, they bunched around the leader and their words sounded frantic; their eyes showed panic.

The Comanche leader appeared to listen to his followers and made the sign to accept the kind offer of the wagons for two cows and two horses. They would take the gifts and go home. Flint extended his right arm to the leader to seal the bargain. The deal was made and they would keep their word.

Flint knew also that the Comanche would go back to their camp and tell about the gun that fired many times and could kill Comanche warriors like a great knife blade against the grass. The Comanche would want some of these guns.

The three-man party returned to the wagons and advised the others of the bargain. Flint caught a glimpse of Johanna watching him intently from the gathered crowd. A glint of admiration gleamed in her eyes.

Two fat cows and two sound horses were selected by lot from the wagon train members and turned out. Comanche riders swooped down from the horizon waving blankets, driving the stock before them. The wagon crowd watched in awe at the superb horsemanship displayed before their eyes. The stock was quickly driven toward the south and within minutes, the Comanche disappeared into the surrounding landscape.

Flint suddenly found himself somewhat in the role of "hero" to the folks of the wagons. He blushed a bit, and a silly grin spread slowly across his face—sort of like a little boy caught with his hand in the cookie jar.

Johanna suddenly appeared by his side, her eyes shining with great admiration for his strength of character and bravery in the face of danger.

Not surprisingly, Elsa McKenna whispered into her husband's ear just then, and smiling, pointed to the couple. Robert McKenna nodded to his wife and stepped forward saying, "Young man, Mr. Stockton. Just what are you intentions toward our daughter?"

Flint looked deeply into Johanna's eyes for a long moment, then turned and answered her father. "I intend to marry your daughter, Sir. I have a deep love for her and do hereby promise that I will love, cherish, and defend her as long as we shall live—if she will have me."

"Then, Flint," Robert McKenna announced, as he gave an approving grin to his eldest daughter, "You will be joined in marriage when Johanna has located her trousseau and is prepared for a ceremony." Johanna caught hold of Flint's arm and squeezed it, showing her delight with her parents' ready consent.

Flint's eyes went wide. He couldn't believe it. Johanna was marrying him. He looked down at her. Raising her face to his gaze, she held the loveliest smile on her face.

CHAPTER THREE

Newly Weds

When everyone agrees that a wedding should occur, only a day is needed to prepare. The wedding of Flint Stockton to Johanna McKenna was quite simple in its format. The "preacher" was really a deacon of sorts but the closest man of God available. By late afternoon, the wagon train boss brought forth a paper that he had quickly composed, and all that witnessed the marriage vows signed the paper. Afterward, "guests" enjoyed Dutch oven cake, coffee, spirits, and dancing to the combination of George Corney's fiddle and Martin Kane's banjo.

That night, Flint Stockton and his bride Johanna spent the night inside the McKenna wagon. The rest of the family slept out under the stars.

A week passed and there was no further sign of the Comanche, or of any other unwanted visitors. Flint and Johanna prepared to leave the wagon train and head north toward the West Texas Plains where they would make their home.

They hadn't a wagon, so all of Johanna's belongings were packed carefully on a second packhorse. After misty-eyed farewells and warm hugs, the newly married couple bid their good-byes and mounted. They struck out toward the north.

At the end of the first day's travel, after the campfire was built and supper prepared, Flint Stockton turned to Johanna and asked, "I know that you can cook. Can you shoot a rifle or pistol?"

Johanna smiled at him and nodded the affirmative. She got up, went to her saddlebags and produced a small flintlock pistol that her father had discreetly given her.

"Father taught me how to load and shoot this."

"Well, Dear. I want to teach you how to load and shoot this new revolving pistol. Your father may have mentioned it in your presence. It is called a Paterson Colt. It has five bullets in this cylinder. Come, I will instruct you in its use."

And so, Johanna got her first lesson on firing a Colt revolver. Flint taught her how to load it, aim it, and fire it by squeezing the trigger instead of jerking or flinching it. He habitually had her practice with the revolver every evening after supper while they traveled.

"That's it, Johanna. Cock back the hammer as you line up on your target. Take a breath and hold it only for an instant. Let out your breath and squeeze the trigger gently. Don't jerk it back."

"Flint, that seems like too much to do in order to shoot. Take a breath and let it out? Shouldn't I be just pointing and shooting it?"

Flint smiled at her. "Just practice as I've shown and talked you through it. It will become second nature to you after a while."

After a week, she had progressed so well that they held their own shooting contest between them. Flint fashioned various types of targets and they would see who could put the most of five bullets into them.

Johanna gave Flint a good run for his money and they laughed about it. Flint was pleased. His young wife could shoot almost as well as he. Next, he showed her his rifle and taught her to shoot it also.

Within a month, Johanna grew into pretty much a marksman, running a very close second to Flint himself. Flint beamed with pride. Out on the frontier, a good wife was a partner to her man, and that also included helping to defend their home against all that would harm them.

Three weeks later, the young couple sat their horses and looked over the land in West Texas. There was a flowing creek, a dense stand of cottonwoods and mesquite, tall grasses, and long sloping, rolling hills. They had found home.

They made camp early that afternoon and, gathering up a multitude of various-sized fallen tree limbs, put together the framework of a lean-to. Tarps from their packhorses lay across the top of the frame to make a temporary shelter from the elements.

Later, Flint fashioned and drove wooden pegs or stakes into the ground to outline their future home. Their first disagreement happened that afternoon. As with most young couples, each had a differing vision of the home they would build together. They bickered as where to place the kitchen, dining, bedroom, and main living area.

"No, Flint. The kitchen area doesn't belong on the west side of our house. It should be on the east side, so that the morning sun greets us at breakfast and helps cool us in the evening when it sets."

"Well then, I will build the fireplace so it is accessible from both the living area and kitchen. The door will be facing south and there will be windows with shutters on each side. There will be a window on each side of the house for safety."

Johanna knew what that meant. There was the distinct probability of Indian raids in their locale since they seemed to be well west of the accepted Texas Frontier. She nodded her head in understanding. When all was said and done, Johanna won the kitchen, dining area and bedroom points. Flint won the main living area and placement of the fireplace.

By sunset, together, they sat down on the sandy clay ground and lay back on their elbows. They looked over the site they had chosen and pondered it. They had the shade of the cottonwood trees, with water close at hand. The house would stand with all four sides open to defense. Johanna even picked out the space where her vegetable garden would go.

Later that evening after a supper of spit-roasted prairie hen and vegetables, they slipped into their blankets beside the softly glowing campfire. It was dark, but the clear night and stars shined brilliantly— seemingly only for them. They lay together and looked deeply into each other's eyes while the smoldering bond of love enveloped them. They drifted off into peaceful slumber.

The next morning, Flint set about to scout the area and map out the parameters of his land. Johanna set about making their camp "home" a bit more comfortable. Flint left one of his Paterson Colts with Johanna, taking his rifle and second revolver with him. Johanna busied herself by gathering a lot of fallen dry wood for their campfire.

Flint returned around one o'clock and, stripping off his shirt, began to dig up clay and sand. Johanna gathered piles of strong grasses with his Bowie knife. The next morning, they began making crude bricks with which to build their home.

The days passed slowly and as the large homemade bricks cured in the West Texas sun, they placed them to form a house. Slick mud from the creek was transformed into homemade mortar, used in between each brick and allowed to dry. The dirt floor was tamped down each evening and over the days became hard. Johanna made a crude broom from thick straws and swept the hard dirt floor every evening.

Flint fashioned the roof by cutting down a few large cottonwoods and splitting them into planks of various sizes. He also fashioned some shingles for the roof and nailed them down overlapping each other.

Two months later, the young couple looked upon the results of their efforts. There stood a strong adobe brick home with shuttered windows on all sides of the house. Johanna cooked in an open hearth with built in Dutch oven that Flint had created to her specifications.

Although there was an abundance of rabbits, prairie hens, antelope, and fish, something seemed to be missing. Johanna was suddenly silent.

"What is it, Johanna? Did we miss something?"

"Yes, Flint. We have got to get some supplies. If ever I'm to bake you my bread, we need flour, yeast, sugar, salt, and such things. We need to find out where the closest trading post or town is, and we need to have a wagon, some more horses, maybe a cow or two. We need other such things as coffee, canned food, and more wood. I'd like to have a nice table and some chairs, just a bit of furniture. Maybe, even a nice bed."

Flint reflected on that.

"You're right, Johanna. I've been so used to sleeping in blankets on the hard floor that I've forgotten that you need your comforts. This is your home. Tomorrow, we'll both ride to the east of here. I recall from my earlier travels that there is a small town, or a trading post within a day's ride. We will find it."

Just as the sun rose in the east, Flint saddled their horses and readied the pack animals. Johanna dressed in a long riding skirt, blouse, and coat. She wore a wide brimmed straw hat to shade her from the unmerciful Texas sun.

Flint led out toward the east. He wore both Paterson Colts and carried his rifle across his saddle pommel. Johanna led the packhorses.

They traveled slow and easy for the first half of the day. It was just after noon that they saw the thin trail of smoke in the distance. Flint pulled up and let Johanna ride alongside of him. He pointed out the smoke.

"Looks like a camp of some sort. We'll ride easy and careful like."

As they neared the camp, they could make out a wagon and five men sitting around a campfire. They appeared to be having their noon meal. Flint reached to his belt and taking out his left-hand revolver, handed it to Johanna.

"Keep this handy under your coat. I don't expect trouble at this point, but it's always good to be ready."

As they drew nearer to the camp, they could make out the features of the five men. They were dirty looking, unkempt, and wore rough dirty clothes. As they looked up from cans of beans and coffee, their eyes locked on Johanna and one of the men smirked and licked his lips as if in anticipation of foul play.

Flint and Johanna drew up well back from the men. Flint leaned slightly forward on his saddle pommel and looked into their eyes. He didn't like what he saw.

"Howdy," said Flint. "Saw your camp. We're traveling to the town east of here. How far would you say it is?"

"Well, now, *friend*, why don't you both light down and have some coffee. We'll talk about that town."

"No. Thank you. Just tell me how far it is and we'll be on our way."

Three of the men slyly looked and grinned at each other. Suddenly, they reached for their weapons and Flint faced the bores of three flintlock pistols. He sat motionless for a long moment contemplating the men's next move.

The seemingly leader of the group suddenly commanded, "Get down offen them hosses. We want to talk with you, and especially with the woman."

Flint could almost feel Johanna shudder at the man's harsh voice. He looked straight at the one who had spoken and replied, "And if we don't?"

"We'll blow you out of the saddle and leave your dead carcass for the wolves. The young woman will come with us."

They grinned with lust at Johanna. She stared back at them with set jaw and determined eyes.

Flint retorted with, "You men put down your guns and we'll leave peaceably, or else."

"Or else, what?" chuckled the leader.

"Or else, I'll kill all five of you and leave your carcasses for the scavengers."

All of the men laughed with evil grins as they cocked back the hammers on their flintlock pistols.

The movements became a blur as both Flint and Johanna's hands flashed for the Paterson Colts at their belts. Orange flame, black powder smoke and hot balls of molten lead spit from the deadly duo of revolvers.

Within fifteen to thirty seconds, all five men lay where they had fallen. Flint and Johanna dismounted and checked each man. They were stone cold dead, and each had fired his one shot from the flintlocks, but missed.

To bury the five men where they lay, the young couple first examined the contents of the wagon, looking for a shovel.

Flint threw back the tarp over the wagon and after a few moments shook his head in disgust, "This looks like wares that someone would pillage from hapless folks. I'd be willing to bet that those men killed and robbed for these things."

Besides a pick and shovel, further examination of the wagon contents yielded a hoard of flour, sugar, salt, potatoes, bacon, jerky, coffee, canned goods, powder, and lead. Enough supplies to last them over a month.

"Johanna, we'll take this wagon and these supplies. They won't be needing them anymore. Should someone come looking for them, like an officer of the law, we'll explain what happened to them."

Johanna nodded silently. She had killed her first man and the enormity of what had just happened finally began to sink in.

Flint immediately understood and took her into his arms. He looked deep into her soul and softly whispered to her, "It needed done, Johanna. Those men were evil. They would have killed me and killed you--after violating you. I would never let them do that, and that is why we had to shoot them."

"I know Flint, I'll be all right. It's just that I've never run across anyone like these men."

"The West is full of men like this, Johanna. That's why I taught you to shoot and shoot well. There may come a day when you will have to defend yourself alone. You did well here today. There's no doubt in my mind that you can handle yourself in a tight situation."

Flint gently touched her cheek with his fingers. She raised her face to him and he kissed her. Her arms slipped around him and they stayed like that for a long moment. Finally, they parted.

"Let's get back to our home, Johanna. I'll look for that town in my travels, so we don't have to ask next time."

They tied their horses to the wagon, hitched up the team and drove it back to their home along the creek. Johanna drove the wagon and Flint gathered and drove the slain men's stock that consisted of saddle horses and a few cattle.

In the month that passed after the shoot out on the prairie, Flint found the small semblance of a town called Schmidt Station about a day's ride to the north. The place, it seemed, was a type of swing station for the freighting business. There was a trading post, livery, stock corrals, and a small "Gasthaus" where there were a few rooms to rent.

They drove the wagon there and met the German family who owned and operated the trading post. The proprietor, of course, was Gunter Schmidt, who along with his wife Greta and daughter Ingrid, worked the trading post store. Their two sons worked the livery and stock corrals, and the gasthaus was operated by friends of theirs who had traveled from Germany with them. Eventually, a stagecoach station was established and Schmidt Station became a stopover for folks traveling west or east. Once a month the Stockton couple would drive to the station and marvel at its growth while they shopped for their needs.

Flint continued to capture wild horses and cattle, and on every trip he would take a few into Schmidt Station to sell for cash money or to trade them for what supplies that they needed. Johanna cherished her monthly visits to the station because Greta and Ingrid would always welcome her to their living quarters for coffee and kuchen, a German coffee cake. They would chat for a few hours about *womanly* things.

CHAPTER FOUR

Jasper Rollins

Only a few weeks had passed when a lone rider appeared in the distance. Flint was away, looking for wild stock.

Johanna watched curiously as the man rode slowly toward their home on a handsome bay horse. She stepped back into the doorway for an instant and picked up the Paterson Colt that Flint always left behind for her. She placed it in her waistband behind her back.

The horseman rode up within ten feet of Johanna. He was ruggedly handsome, with flashing dark eyes and a dark-haired brushy mustache that held just a hint of gray. His dark hair was worn long in the fashion of the plainsmen. Rumpled dark trousers were tucked into calf -high leather boots with large rowled silver Mexican spurs. His shirt was of a homespun red material. He wore a faded yellow bandana loosely tied around his neck. A buckskin jacket hung over the back of his saddle along with heavily stuffed saddlebags.

Of particular note was the manner in which he wore two low slung Paterson Colt revolvers. A large Bowie knife was sheathed behind his belt. He also carried what appeared to be a large bore revolving rifle.

The traveler smiled at Johanna with friendly eyes. Johanna looked deep into this man's eyes. She saw honor and justice. He seemed a friendly sort.

"Good afternoon, Ma'am. I'm Jasper Rollins, a Texas Ranger. I wonder if you might spare some water for my horse and maybe, for myself, a bit of that coffee I smell. I've been out on the trails for quite some time and I shore do miss my small comforts."

"Please, Mr. Rollins, dismount and water your horse. I am Johanna Stockton. I'll get you a cup of coffee. Do you take sugar or milk?"

"No. Thank you. Out on the trails it's awful hard to keep up with the pleasures of sugar and such. I'd drink it straight. Did you say your name was Stockton?"

"Yes."

"Your husband wouldn't happen to be Flint Stockton would he, Ma'am?"

"Why, yes, he is."

"I rode with a Flint Stockton during the Battle of San Jacinto. We shore did it to them Mexicans. Both of us were there to see Santa Anna surrender to Sam Houston. I wonder if your husband is the same Flint Stockton."

"Flint should be back sometime later in the day. He told me some about San Jacinto and days after. I will get you some coffee."

Johanna turned to go into the house and Jasper Rollins suddenly broke out in a big wide grin. He saw the Paterson Colt neatly tucked behind her back, ready at hand.

"Bet that it is the Flint Stockton that I know. Also, bet that he taught her and she can use that Colt something fierce," he thought.

Johanna brought him a cup of coffee and two freshly baked cinnamon rolls. She smiled as his eyes lit up with pure pleasure. She also provided him a few large carrots from her small vegetable garden for his horse.

Johanna waited until he had devoured the first cinnamon roll and gulped down half a cup of coffee before she spoke, "What brings you out to this lonely land, Mr. Rollins?"

"Well, Johanna. I was tracking the doings of a group of five desperadoes, well known for murder, ravaging womenfolk, and thievery. Suddenly, yesterday, I came across five lonely graves out on the prairie and I wondered about that. I dug them up and low and behold I find all five of the men that I was a-hunting. I found some worn old wagon tracks in the dirt and thought that I would follow them a while. Well, them tracks just petered out a few miles back, but I kept on riding this direction, just out of curiosity, I suppose." He went on, "You wouldn't happen to know anything about them dead men would you, Johanna?"

Johanna's face flushed and she appeared a bit embarrassed.

"I can wait here for your husband to return if you so wish. Then the three of us can speak of it."

"I'd like that, Mr. Rollins."

"Fine, Johanna. If you don't mind, I'll just make myself comfortable over there under the cottonwood trees. It's been a long time since I've dangled my feet in some cool running creek water. Might even fish a bit. Do you like trout, Johanna?"

"Why, yes, Mr. Rollins. We do like trout."

"Well, maybe I can catch us a mess of trout for supper, that is if you and your husband wouldn't mind company."

"We'd be pleased to have company."

Johanna watched as Jasper Rollins unsaddled his horse and walked down toward the creek bed. The horse just walked along with him and it seemed like he was talking to it as they walked, like they were good friends. She thought she heard him say, "Come on, Sonnet. Let's go fishing."

Flint arrived home with the fading sun to find Johanna cooking up a fine batch of fresh bread and rolls. "What's the occasion? This ain't Sunday, is it?"

"No, Flint. But, there is company. He's down at the creek fishing. He says that he is a Texas Ranger, trailing those five men we killed. He wants to talk about it, but said that he would wait for you to come home."

"A Texas Ranger, huh?"

"Yes. His name is Jasper Rollins."

"Jasper? Ole Jasper from San Jacinto? Ole Jasper from the Texas Cavalry? Where is he?" With each question, Flint's face lit up further with anxious delight.

"Down to the creek, Flint."

Flint Stockton dashed out the door and ran down to the creek. Within moments Johanna heard the most God-awful racket that she could ever imagine.

"Ya-hoo, He-Haw, Yo-o-o-o, Remember the Alamo!"

Five minutes later Flint and Jasper Rollins strode up to the house. Each grinned from ear to ear, and Jasper had a string of twelve beautiful trout. His horse Sonnet trailed him to the hitching rack and stood there. Jasper turned and looked at his horse. "Sonnet, go and lay down for a while. Make yourself comfortable, we'll be here for the night."

The horse turned, trotted over to the cottonwoods, suddenly lay down and rolled lazily around in the tall grasses.

Flint turned to Johanna. "Johanna, this here was my best friend in the Texas Cavalry. He is now a Texas Ranger--the law hereabouts. We'll tell him of those five men."

Jasper Rollins listened intently while the young couple told their story over a supper of pan-fried fish, potatoes, wild scallions, tender cooked carrots, fresh baked rolls, honey, and a pot of freshly brewed, full flavored, coffee.

When they finished, Jasper looked at both of them with admiration. "Them boys were hell on wheels when it came to scrapping with flintlocks. The Paterson Colt really put them down. That's why I carry two of them myself. Mark my words, the Colt Revolver will make a name for itself in the West. Anyway, you two did Texas a great favor by ridding the country of that scum. The Republic of Texas has a reward posted for them boys and I will see that you get it. I do suppose that a young couple like you could use, say, about one thousand dollars?"

"You kidding us, Jasper?"

"No. I'm not funning, Flint. The total reward on them boys is one thousand dollars, dead or alive. You can keep the spoils that you found with them. You say that Johanna nailed two of them? That is some almighty good shooting—especially for a woman. Johanna, you are fast becoming a true Woman of the West. Any good man would give his right arm to have a good wife that can cook like you, and shoot like you. I'm right proud to know you."

Johanna blushed a bit, but breathed a lot easier then, and in the back of her mind formed the thought—"I'm sure glad Flint took the time to teach me."

"By the way, Flint, Johanna, I should be riding through here every couple of months or so. I would shore like to water my hoss and partake of your kind hospitality when I do."

"You are welcome anytime, Jasper," Flint assured his old friend while Johanna nodded her agreement.

*   *   *

True to his word, Jasper Rollins stopped in at the rate of at least once every two months. During the second month after meeting Johanna, he rode into the small ranch yard beaming like the cat that swallowed the canary. He carried a small leather pouch hidden in his saddlebags.

Over a dinner of roasted prairie chicken, mashed potatoes, tender snap beans, chicken gravy, hot flaky biscuits, strawberry jam, and hot coffee, that Jasper suddenly *remembered* his reason for stopping in at the Stockton homestead. "I just happen to have a little something for ya'll." He reached into his shirt and dropped a tanned hide pouch on the table. He motioned to it with his fork while smiling at Johanna. "Well, Johanna, go ahead, open the pouch."

Johanna reached over and pulling the drawstrings, spread the pouch open. Her eyes went wide with disbelief. The pouch contained one thousand dollars in Republic of Texas "Red Backs," the legal tender of Texas at this time.

Jasper roared with laughter, and his eyes sparkled with obvious delight.

"I wanted to see your face when you opened that pouch, Johanna. That look on your face, Johanna, was worth all the time and effort I put into hornswaggling the usual bank draft into cash money for you. Shucks, I told them folks back in Austin that there weren't no bank out here for ya'll to cash that paper and I wanted you folks paid in real spending money. Ya'll enjoy that now, that is, after you pass me some more of that delicious roast chicken."

Flint and Johanna now had more money than they had ever seen in their lives. Jasper had himself a good old time just putting ideas into their minds as to how to use that money: "Why with reputable friends like me coming to visit every now and then, you ought to at least get some good wood and make some comfortable beds. Now I ain't complaining none. That makeshift bed is all right. It's a damn sight better than sleeping in the stable with Sonnet."

Jasper grinned a bit while he contemplated his next sentence. "But, a man and a woman has got to have a comfortable place to—well, you know, just be together."

Both Flint and Johanna turned to look at Jasper with questioning eyes. Whatever did he mean? The light suddenly dawned as a small gleam in both of their eyes. Jasper excused himself to "go and check on my hoss."

When Jasper returned, Johanna asked him, "Why did you call your horse, Sonnet?"

"I thought that you'd never ask. I call him Sonnet because he is like poetry in motion when he gets up and running."

Jasper spent the night in the stable, but was in the kitchen with first light and the first wisp of wood smoke from the chimney. "Johanna, you shore make a good breakfast. A man gets mighty tired of beef jerky and cold biscuits on the trails. That coffee is real good. Sometime when I ride through, could you find it in your heart to make my favorite supper?"

"What is it, Jasper?"

"A beefsteak so thick that you need a sword to cut it. A passel of bacon fried potatoes, thick brown gravy, cobbed corn, flaky biscuits, and a lot of strawberry jam. Honey will do in a pinch."

"Well, Jasper. If we can get it, we'll have it," Johanna promised.

CHAPTER FIVE

Johanna's Surprise

It was six months later that Flint was two days overdue from riding the wild horse trails. Johanna worried because he should have returned long ago. She continually looked toward the distance in all directions. There was no movement—not even a small dust devil. Johanna was also feeling queezy in the stomach each morning. She hadn't said anything to Flint because she didn't want him to worry about her.

Toward evening, she finally saw the slow-moving dot come out of the west. She watched it with growing anticipation. The dot grew into a horseman dragging something behind him. The vision got larger until she finally recognized Jasper Rollins pulling a makeshift travois behind him.

They pulled up in front of the house and Johanna's heart took a leap. Flint lay on the travois bandages up all around his chest. The bandages were bloody. He had been shot, more than once.

Jasper Rollins fairly leaped off Sonnet and hurried back to Flint. He tenderly picked Flint's lanky frame up from the litter and told Johanna to clear the bed. Johanna turned toward the doorway without questions and pulled the quilts and blankets down on their bed. Jasper carried Flint into the house and laid him gently on the bed.

"I found him lying face down in the grass. Comanches, I believe. There were several arrows here and there. They took his horse, guns, and belongings, but left him to die on the prairie. He must've fought them bravely for them not to want to scalp him. Any-ways, I brung him home. I took two bullets out've him and he will be down for a few weeks. I will stick around and help out until he can get up and walk." Johanna nodded affirmatively while she stared at her unconscious husband.

"I shore could use a good cup of coffee right now," Jasper tiredly spoke.

Johanna turned to him, with gratitude shining in her eyes. "You can have all the coffee you want, Jasper, and tomorrow, I will cook you the biggest beefsteak I can find. You brought him home."

Jasper studied Johanna for a long minute, "You been sickly in the mornings, huh?"

"How did you know that, Jasper?"

"Well, I've known you for quite a while now, Johanna. Your complexion is rosy and there is a certain glow about you. The way you move, the way you look. Yes, it's there."

"Whatever are you babbling about, Jasper? Just come out and say it."

"Johanna. You are going to have a baby."

Johanna was dumbfounded. She was going to have a baby. She was going to have a baby, and Jasper Rollins realized it before she did.

"Don't look so surprised, Johanna. I have known many a good woman, and somehow I can spot their condition within a very few minutes. No, don't worry. I won't tell Flint. That's your job. I can hardly wait to see what the little critter will be. I'd shore like to have me a little fishing partner."

"Well, Jasper. If I am going to have a baby, I hope that it is a boy. Flint needs a son to teach all that he knows."

"Johanna, I'll stop back in about two to three months. One look and I'll tell you what it is. I ain't been too awful wrong all these years. Hell, Johanna, if it's a boy, I'll cook you a big beefsteak. If it's a girl, I'll buy her the prettiest doll I can find in the entire Republic of Texas."

*　　　*　　　*

Six months later Jasper Rollins rode onto the Stockton homestead and grinned at Johanna. She was radiant but waddling. Jasper watched her thoughtfully, "Flint, from now on, you've got to help out all you can. Watch her closely, because you will never know when that little critter is going to want to show himself to the world. Matter of fact Johanna, I think that your baby will arrive sometime around the middle of December."

*   *   *

A mid-December blizzard had blown in during the night and Flint was out seeing to their stock. Johanna was putting the beginnings on a fine stew when the first pain hit. She flinched and her eyes went wide. It lasted only a few moments but it was sharp and intense. She massaged her belly and the pain seemed to ease a bit.

Ten minutes later another extremely sharp pain surged through her and she almost fell to her knees. Johanna closed her eyes and gritted her teeth. Suddenly, she knew what was happening. She was about to give birth all alone.

Johanna put on her tea kettle. She stoked the flames of the stove to flaming hot. She moved slowly to their bed and sat down. She removed her undergarments and sat there with her eyes closed for a long moment. She felt a slight tremor, a slight movement that seemed to shiver all the way down to her toes.

The next pain came, causing Johanna to shriek out. She wormed her way onto the bed, and grasped the rawhide rope that she had fashioned just for this task. She placed it between her teeth and lay waiting for the next pain. A moment later another pain began and built to near unbearable intensity throughout her body.

Suddenly, the door swung open and Jasper Rollins stood there in front of Johanna. "Where's Flint?" he asked, and when she replied through gritted teeth, he shook his head up and down for a moment, then unbuckled his gunbelt and let it drop to the floor. Next, he rolled up his sleeves.

He moved to the stove and made sure of the hot water. He dipped out some to wash his hands. He moved to Johanna and took her small hand into his big burly, rough hands. He held her hand gently and he began to speak in soft tones.

"Johanna. It is time. You are going to have that sweet little baby. Think of it, a little tiny baby. I am here with you, and together, we will do this. Now, once upon a time there was a great and handsome Ranger. He rode a mangy hoss and called it "Dog". One day the hoss had enough of this and when the Ranger tried to mount it, it side stepped and the Ranger fell into a big pile of hoss—stuff."

Johanna started to laugh. She laughed hard and it hurt. Suddenly the pain was excruciating. She felt the downward movement as the baby suddenly eased toward the birth canal. It was time.

Jasper held Johanna's hand and softly spoke to her as contractions slowly birthed the child she had carried for so long.

Finally Jasper moved to the foot of the bed. He swallowed hard and taking his large hands held the head and shoulders of the child and told Johanna, "PUSH as hard as you can."

Minutes ticked by and then Johanna sighed a long and tired breath. The sound of a quick slap followed with a baby's wail and her eyes went wide. Jasper moved over her and gently laid the newborn on her chest. Johanna wept with joy.

An hour later, the door to the Stockton house opened and a near frozen Flint Stockton stiffly moved to the iron stove for the heat. He shivered violently as he stood there.

Jasper suddenly appeared out of the bedroom and he had the biggest and silliest grin that Flint had ever seen. "Frozen up a bit, huh? Well, Flint, I got something that will warm your gizzard. Come with me."

Jasper took Flint's icy cold hand and led him to Johanna. Flint looked down at the baby nursing at Johanna's breast and then into her eyes. She held the most beautiful look that he had ever seen.

"Flint. Come look. This is our son."

"What's his name?"

"Well, I would like to call him Robert after my father. We can call him Colter after your father. Robert Colter Stockton. Yes. Is that all right with you, Flint?"

"Well, let's shorten that a bit. Let's call him Robert Cole Stockton. Until he reaches the right age, we can call him Bobby Cole. That does have sort of a ring to it."

"Yes, Flint," Johanna agreed. Then softly looking at her son, she said, "Bobby Cole Stockton, this is your father."

Flint Stockton reached down with trembling hands and took the small child from Johanna. He held it to his own chest and felt the small heart beating against his own. He closed his eyes and tears rolled down his wind-burned cheeks. He swallowed hard.

"Johanna, he is beautiful. I love you so much. How can I help you?"

"Shucks, Flint," interrupted Jasper laughing, "you can sit there by her side all day bug-eyed and such. Don't you worry about nothing. I'll cook ya'll a meal tonight to end all meals. I hope you both like beef, beans, and biscuits, because that's all I know how to cook."

And thus on a cold December day a child soon to be known to the West as Cole Stockton was born. His father looked down upon him and said softly to himself, "I'll teach you the way of the West. I'll teach you the gun. I'll teach you to hunt, fish, and gather wild stock. You are my son and I love you."

Johanna Stockton looked lovingly at her son and held him close to her breast. She thought to herself, "I am glad that you are a son. My husband needs a son to teach the ways of the West. You'll grow to be strong in mind, in character and I'll teach you schooling. A man needs to have some book learning. You will think a lot and you will know a lot. Both of us will be proud of you—Bobby Cole Stockton."

CHAPTER SIX

Bobby Cole

In the years that followed, Robert Cole Stockton grew to be tall and lanky like his father. He had sandy-colored hair and bluish-green eyes that changed hue with his mood. He was curious about everything. His parents could see the silent wheels of his mind turning when they looked deep into his eyes after they answered his many questions.

Flint began to teach his son about the animals and nature in general at around five years old, and Bobby Cole learned fast. With lessons over for the day, Flint would take him to the creek bank and with homemade fishing pole in hand, both would dangle their feet into the clear cool water and laze back just watching the clouds float by. They had many fine talks like that.

On occasion, whenever Jasper Rollins visited, the three of them would sit quietly along the bank and fish. Jasper would tell tall tales and the trio laughed a lot.

It was during one of these visits that Jasper looked closely at Johanna and grinned. She caught the look and her eyes went wide. She shook her head "No." He shook his head "Yes."

Flint caught the silent signals between them and inquired, "What are you two talking about?"

"Well, tell him, Johanna."

"Jasper thinks that I am having another baby."

"You are? We are going to have another baby?"

"I don't think so, Flint."

"I know so," said a grinning Jasper. "Now don't say I didn't warn you, Johanna. Remember the last time? When Old Jasper says that a woman is going to have a baby, she shore enough has one. Besides, you got that look again."

"But, I haven't been sickly in the mornings like last time."

"Sometimes, Johanna, a woman don't get sickly like that after the first child. But, mark my words. You are with child."

*   *   *

Four weeks later when Johanna noticed that she was constantly hungry. "Goodness. I haven't eaten like this since before Bobby Cole was born." The thought suddenly struck her. "Well, I'll be. I'm with child. I can sense it."

Two months later, Johanna was showing and she looked lovely. Her complexion was radiant.

About that time, Jasper Rollins rode up and stayed the night with them. "Told you so, Johanna. Old Jasper ain't never been wrong on matters of the heart nor on matters of nature. I'll try to be here when this little critter comes also."

Johanna shook her head smiling, "I hope I don't need you. I intend to keep Flint closer to home this time."

In the fall of the year, five months later, Jasper Rollins arrived at the Stockton home and found that the newest Stockton had already arrived: Clayton Allen Stockton whom folks would call Clay Stockton.

On Bobby Cole Stockton's eighth birthday, his father unloaded his Patterson Colt revolver and handed it to him. He told him, "Bobby Cole. You're soon to be a young man. I want you to take this revolver and learn it from the tip of the barrel to the end of the handle grips. When you're ready, come to me and we'll talk further."

A week later, Bobby Cole Stockton came to his father. "I know this gun by its feel and can tell you all about it."

That afternoon, Bobby Cole Stockton and his father stood at the creek bed and fired their revolvers at makeshift targets. Johanna listened intently to the banging of the revolvers and recalled her own lessons from Flint with a slight smile on her face.

About the time Bobby Cole neared twelve years old, Jasper Rollins rode up to the Stockton home and asked Flint to help him track down some Comancheros. Flint turned to Bobby Cole, told him, "You'll be the man of the family until I return. It shouldn't be more than four or five days." Flint rode out with Jasper Rollins toward the Southwest.

Two days later Johanna was hanging out laundry and humming softly to herself. Bobby Cole Stockton came urgently running up from the creek and shouted to his mother, "Quick! Get inside the house and board up all the windows."

Johanna looked quickly toward the creek. About twenty Comanche warriors were crossing the creek and fanning out to surround the house. She dashed into the house and began slamming and barring all the windows. Bobby Cole took the long flintlock rifle down from over the fireplace and loaded it. He got the shotgun from the corner behind the door and also loaded it. He slammed and barred the heavy wooden door.

Johanna got her revolver and also the flintlock pistol that her father had given her and made sure that both were loaded. She grabbed up the four year old Clay Stockton and placed him behind the heavy overturned kitchen table and told him, "There's gonna be a lot of noise but don't cry. She gave him his toy horse and Clay felt reassured.

Johanna stood at the rear of the house and peered through the loop holes in the heavy shutters. She could see no movement. She looked toward the front of the house. She watched as Bobby Cole calmly opened the cylinder of the Paterson Colt and checked the loads.

Suddenly, the wild screams of the Comanche signaled their attack. She saw Bobby Cole ease his revolver to the slot at the window and methodically fire. Eerie screams sounded as hot lead thunked into sun-browned bodies.

Johanna suddenly heard chopping sounds at the back of the house. "They're trying to axe open the back shutters!" she yelled and dashed to that room.

Three shots cracked out in quick succession from her revolver, and two Comanche dropped dead to the ground. The third lurched away holding his stomach.

Bobby Cole Stockton emptied his revolver, then quickly slid the cylinder pin and dropped the empty cylinder to his pocket. He took up a fully loaded cylinder and slipped it into the housing, then slid the pin back into place as five warriors pushed the heavy wagon toward the door as a battering ram.

Comanche warriors were within twenty feet of the door when Bobby Cole squeezed off the first of five shots. Of the five Comanche with the wagon, two of them died instantly shot through the chest, one took lead in his side, another crawled off with a bullet in his upper thigh. The other two warriors helped their wounded friends. Blood covered the ground.

A silence followed, and Johanna breathed hard. It was stifling inside the house from the West Texas heat. Sweat trickled down her neck and between her breasts, and her blouse clung to her torso.

She turned and looked into Bobby Cole's eyes. She saw for the first time, the hard determination on his face and for just an instant, the sudden flash of soul-burning hell fire. She shivered as the realization shook through her. She thought, "Bobby Cole is a natural with that gun. Look how he holds that revolver—like its part of him. He's quick and sure. He just stands there, watching and waiting. Look how alert he is. He hears every sound and moves to meet them."

For two days the Stockton family held their house against the Comanche. During the night, no fire was lit inside the house. They ate jerky with cold bread and drank tepid water from a keg that Johanna kept near the cupboards. Only Clay seemed to sleep.

Toward the next early afternoon, ammunition was dwindling. There were only five rounds of revolver left and the shotgun and rifle ammunition was gone. Only the flintlock pistol had not been fired.

Bobby Cole Stockton turned to his mother and gently took the flintlock pistol from her hand. He checked the load and slipped it into his belt. He led her to the table where Clay lay napping and bid her to lie there also. He then stood in front of the overturned table and waited.

Within minutes, all remaining Comanche, moved to the front of the house. Flaming arrows pounded into the heavy wooden door and it began to burn. Smoke filled the house and Johanna tied wet bandanas over her own and Clay's face. Bobby Cole already had one over his face. He stood there, eyes watering from the smoke and weapons at the ready.

The door blazed intensely, then, crashed inward. Three warriors jumped through, screaming their death cries into the house. Three shots cracked immediately, and they slammed back as if they were hit with a hammer. All three took rounds in the chest at not more than six feet.

Bobby Cole Stockton stood motionless with both the Paterson Colt and flintlock pistol cocked and ready for the final moment. It never came. The remaining Comanche suddenly disappeared and within minutes, Johanna and Bobby Cole knew the reason why.

A company of twenty Rangers boiled hell-bent-for-leather into the Stockton front yard; Flint and Jasper Rollins among them.

Flint Stockton leaped from his horse and dashed frantically through the charred doorframe and into his home. He found Bobby Cole holding both pistols cocked at the ready with Johanna and Clay behind the over-turned table. He gathered them all up in his arms and held them tightly. Once again his lessons had paid off in saving the lives of those he held dearly.

Flint, Jasper, and the Rangers all listened to Johanna's account of the attack, and especially of the actions taken by their son, Bobby Cole Stockton.

Later, when finally alone, Johanna appraised Flint of the instant flash in Bobby Cole's eyes. "He stood there and shot them, Flint. He is fast and steady. There was a certain look in his eyes. Just for an instant, I could almost feel the intensity of, well, like the fire of his soul, and it made me shiver. He has the knack for guns and the willingness to use them."

"He's become a man, Johanna. He may only be almost twelve years old, but there stands a man. He has fought the Comanche and killed his first man. There can be no other way. He must be treated like a young man. Here in the West, when a boy becomes a man, he deserves respect. We'll teach him right from wrong. We must continue to teach him honor, justice, and fairness. He'll grow to be strong, and one day, he'll make a name for himself in the West."

*　　　*　　　*

It was nearing 1861 when Flint Stockton looked at his side arms and decided that it was time for a change. After all, the Paterson Colt was outmoded. It held only a five shot cylinder, and now the Colt Firearms Company had introduced the Colt Army Model 1860, a six-shot revolver of the .44 caliber.

Flint rode to the nearest town with a gunsmith and bought himself four Colt Army 1860 revolvers as well as related munitions. It would be a Christmas to be remembered in the Stockton family.

He also bought himself a Colt Revolving Shotgun, caliber .75. He was proud. He would provide the means of defense to all of his family members.

Christmas afternoon, 1860, found Flint, Johanna, Cole, and Clay Stockton all facing homemade targets across the creek at approximately thirty yards. This was a brand new lesson for *all* of the Stocktons.

Flint grinned a bit, then lined up on his target. He squeezed the trigger. The resounding crack of the .44 was louder and more pronounced than the Paterson Colt that they had been carrying for so long.

Flint couldn't believe it. He missed the target entirely. His bullet burst up dust just the other side of the large food tin. He started to line up again when sixteen-year-old Bobby Cole gently touched him on the shoulder.

Flint looked into the questioning eyes of his eldest son and nodded. They had agreed beforehand to only one practice shot to line up before the Stockton family shoot out.

The winner could name the next day's supper and have it served to him, or her, like a fancy restaurant.

Bobby Cole Stockton cocked his brand new Army Colt .44 revolver. He drew a deep breath, held it for only a second, then exhaled half of it. He squeezed the trigger. The half gallon can burst high into the air—shot clean at exactly the center.

Johanna was next. She copied Bobby Cole in her mannerism, except, that she turned to Flint Stockton with a devilish grin and laughed slightly. She took only a second. The Colt lined up on her target, she squeezed off, and the tin flew into the air.

Flint felt dumbfounded. He had bought these revolvers for each of his family members and they were literally out shooting him. This fact dumbfounded him.

Next, a young Clay held his revolver to the ready. Flint watched his eyes. Clay fired, and missed the tin—barely. His round sailed into the dirt exactly next to the can.

"Don't worry, Clay" said Flint, "you'll do better next time. Well now, let the shooting match begin."

Each of the Stockton family had one half-gallon empty food tin to shoot. Whoever would put six out of six bullets into his or her target would be the winner.

Four Colt Army revolvers shattered the air, blasting away at each target. After six rounds from each family member, the family moved forward to survey the results.

Flint couldn't believe it. Johanna had fired a perfect six bullets into her can. Clay had fired three out of six into his can; Flint himself had fired four of six with two rounds barely missing the can. He shook his head and went to the next can—the one shot by Bobby Cole.

Flint looked hard at that can and swallowed the lump that suddenly appeared in his throat. There was only ONE HOLE in that can. But, the hole was spread like six bullets had whizzed through it and each one had nipped off another bit of the edge. Bobby Cole, it seemed, had put six bullets into a small pattern to the point that it was impossible to determine just how many bullets had passed through it.

Flint exhaled a long breath of air. Bobby Cole had a knack for the gun all right. He fired precisely and he was fast. He was "born to the gun," so-to-speak, as the old timers phrased it. Flint swallowed his pride and just shook his head. His entire family had relatively outshot him.

Just to add insult to injury, Johanna stepped up to him, kissed him lightly on the cheek and advised him to "seek out lessons" from Bobby Cole. "I did," she teased, "and they seemed to work. I mean, Flint, you were great with the weapons of your time, but Bobby Cole seems to have the *feel* for these newer Colts. Please don't take it so hard. After all, it was you that taught him in the first place. He wouldn't have all of this knowledge, if you hadn't taught him. Now, it seems that it's his turn to teach you. Remember what you first said to me? Let me remind you."

She recounted from memory, "I'm going to teach you something that may save your life. You may already know how to use a firearm, but this one is different. You'll have to learn it from the tip of the bore to the end of the handle. It'll become *one* with you." Johanna smiled warmly. "Go to him, Flint, and ask Bobby Cole to teach you this new firearm."

Flint Stockton swallowed his pride and served supper to all three of his family. Later, in the evening when the sun was disappearing over the edge of the earth, he turned to his son, Bobby Cole, and asked him to *guide* him in the use of the new firearms. "Bobby Cole, you showed us all your skill and knowledge of this new Colt revolver today. I would like you to show me more about it. Guide me to know it well."

Bobby Cole Stockton swallowed hard. "I get to show you? My father? Are you sure? You're the man that showed me?"

"Yes, Bobby Cole. I want you to show me everything that you know about this new Colt .44, Army. I want to be the best that I can."

Only three days later, Johanna heard the constant crack of revolver fire and knew that her husband had learned well from their son. They were engaged in another friendly shoot out. Clay appeared and stood beside his Mother. He had that *grin* on his face.

"Got us some supper, Ma. This here rabbit was over fifty yards when I nailed him. I seem to be getting a lot better with the rifle. Cole dearly loves that revolver that he got for Christmas. I like mine also, but I like the rifle a lot better."

"What did you say, Clay?"

"I like the rifle a lot better."

"No. Before that."

"Let's see. I said that Cole dearly loves that revolver."

"That's it! Why did you call your brother, Cole?"

"He told me that I could. I hate the name Bobby. It sounds so, well, like a little kid. My brother is not a little kid. I like him and he shows me things. I think its better; now that he is all grown up, his name should be Cole Stockton."

Johanna Marie Stockton reflected on this name change and before retiring for the night, after thanking Flint for the well prepared beef, beans, and biscuits meal, she spoke softly into his ear. "Cole Stockton."

Flint Stockton sat straight up in the bed and he held a very inquisitive look on his face.

"Now, that rings a bell. Were you perchance speaking with our youngest son?"

"Yes, Flint, and I agree. Bobby is a name that reeks of youth. Our son is by no means a youth. He is a man. You said that yourself back a few years ago. Ask him, Flint. What does Bobby Cole want to be called?"

"I don't have to ask, Johanna. I already know. His name is Cole Stockton from now on."

"There is a good ring to that, Flint. I know that he will forge a name for himself, but I also know that he will forge a name of HONOR for the entire Stockton family. Trust me. One day, our son will be famous. I feel it in my heart.

CHAPTER SEVEN

Dawn of the Gunfighter

In the spring of the following year, Jasper Rollins once again came riding into the Stockton ranch yard. He looked worn and tired.

Flint was out on the range tending stock, and Jasper had a situation that couldn't wait for Flint to return. There were four desperate men that he was hunting and their trail led to just north of the Stockton homestead.

Jasper asked if the seventeen-year-old Cole Stockton could help him track down and capture those men. "It shouldn't be too awful dangerous," Jasper assured Johanna. "we can sneak up on them during the night and take them without much of a struggle in the early hours of the morning. Should be pretty quick."

Johanna agreed to let Cole join Jasper in Flint's absence. They rode out together within the half hour. As she returned to her chores, an image, rather a thought, suddenly flashed across Johanna's mind. She could almost envision a wounded man lying on the ground and another fighting for his life amongst dark shadows that were shooting from everywhere. A shudder of dread ran through her body.

Jasper Rollins and Cole Stockton rode quietly through gullies that paralleled the outlaws' hiding place. The sun was just a sliver of light as it moved down over the horizon. Then, darkness shrouded the land. The moon had not yet risen and the going was slow and careful.

By the early hours just before dawn, Jasper and Cole were in position. They lay on the ground about thirty yards from each other and facing the outlaw camp. Each held his pistol ready.

Just as the dawn slowly broke over the horizon, the outlaw who stood watch during the night reached over and tossed a good sized-log on the fire. It blazed up. He picked up the coffee pot and as he turned to his canteen for water, he suddenly saw Jasper rise up from the ground.

"Texas Ranger! Drop your guns and grab sky!"

The outlaw fancied himself a fast draw and as he moved to unbuckle his gunbelt, he drew and leveled his revolver at Jasper. Jasper squeezed off his own Colt at the same time, and each was hit by the other.

The outlaw never knew what hit him. Jasper's bullet smacked into his heart. Jasper was hit high in the chest and he slammed to the ground, unmoving.

The other three outlaws jumped to their feet drawing their weapons as they did. They saw their partner fall dead and the Ranger slam backward. They started toward Jasper with drawn and cocked revolvers.

"Make sure that damn Ranger is dead."

Suddenly, Cole stood up to the side of them, Colt revolver in hand and a determined look on his face.

"Damn, another one. Let's smoke him down."

Cole immediately shot the tall one on the far right in the chest, then turned his gun on the short one to the left. The bullet whizzed through the man's shirt sleeve and pillowed up dirt the other side of him.

The center man fired at Cole and the bullet tore through Cole's baggy shirt around the waist. Cole pointed his revolver and shot the man point blank in his paunchy stomach. The man doubled over in wrenching pain as the hot fire burned in his gut.

The short remaining outlaw went crazy. He moved toward Cole Stockton, gun blazing. Cole stood his ground and taking careful aim, and shot the man dead center in the chest. The outlaw slammed backward with the first round, his eyes wide with disbelief that a skinny kid could shoot like that. The second bullet caught him an inch lower than the first, and the third tore through his right cheek to exit the back of his skull. The outlaw jerked straight back and fell to the ground. All four of the outlaws were dead.

Cole moved quickly to Jasper and examined him. He was out cold and bleeding. Cole went to Jasper's saddlebags and grabbed up his spare shirt. He tore it into strips and wadded a large piece into a compress. He placed it snugly against the wound, then bound it securely in place with the strips of cloth.

That bullet had to come out and Cole had never done anything like that before. He must get Jasper to the Stockton homestead. Flint and Johanna would know what to do.

Cole rigged a travois to Jasper's horse, then dragged the fallen Ranger to it. He rolled Jasper's heavy frame onto the litter, then used his rope to secure him to it.

Next, Cole gathered up the dead men and after saddling their horses, laid the bodies over their saddles and tied them on. He smothered out their camp fire with handfuls of dirt, and the remnants of their coffee. He then mounted his own dun-colored horse and turned toward the Stockton home, leading a string of horses with the wounded Jasper and four dead outlaws.

*   *   *

It was close to noon when Johanna stood at the clothes line. She heard a horse whinny and looked up. Her face turned pale as she recognized her son Cole leading five horses and a travois. They pulled into the yard as Johanna yelled for Flint and Clay to come and help.

"Never mind those men over the saddles, they're all dead," said Cole. "Jasper's been hurt bad. There's a bullet that needs to come out. I would have done it, but I don't know how. I brought him straight here."

They carried Jasper into the house and laid him gently across the kitchen table. Johanna put water on the stove to heat up. Flint examined the wound, "It's bad. I'll have to dig out the bullet. I'll need help, Johanna. The boys can start burying those dead outlaws. Cole, see if there is any whiskey in any of those saddlebags."

Flint turned to Johanna's kitchen wares and, taking two of her sharpest knives, began to sharpen them further on a whetstone. Within a few minutes both knives cut like razors. He dropped the knives into the boiling water, then pulled them out with a pair of tongs.

Cole found a bottle of whiskey in the pack of one outlaw and brought it to Flint. Flint poured whiskey all over Jasper's wound. Jasper never flinched. He was out cold. Flint took a deep breath and began to cut into the Ranger's chest along the path of the bullet. Flint and Johanna worked side by side to save the Ranger's life. Flint cut and dug for the bullet, and Johanna swabbed the blood away with clean rags so that Flint could see what he was doing.

Toward sundown, Flint and Johanna finally put Jasper to bed with fresh bandages and made him swallow a few sips of whiskey.

It was not until then that they asked Cole about the gunfight.

"There isn't much to tell. Jasper and one outlaw shot each other. The others shot at me and I shot them."

Clay suddenly spoke up. "Yah, and one of those men had two bullets in his chest in a small circle about this size with a third bullet in his jaw." He held his hand up with his thumb and forefinger together. It was about the size of a silver dollar.

Flint Stockton reflected on his younger son's last comment. Cole had shot that man three times. He suddenly knew that it was a fight for life, and Cole stood his ground with bullets flying all around him. Cole had the makings of a real *gunfighter*.

*   *   *

Jasper Rollins took months to recover from his wounds and with that much time to consider his future, decided to resign from the Rangers. He had enough of killing and being the target for everything that moved. With Johanna's help, Jasper penned a letter to the Ranger headquarters in Austin explaining his decision. Afterward, he bid his farewell and moved on toward the New Mexico Territory where all he had to worry about was outlaws, Apaches, and rough men that would draw weapons at the drop of a hat.

Cole, it seemed, would prove his skill again and again. During the Civil War, many a man fled to the West to avoid conscription into the armies of both North and South. The War touched Texas, and many sons of the Republic sent their sons into battle against the North. Many would die, but they served bravely.

Cole never served in either army. When U.S Cavalry units left Texas to support the Union cause in the Civil War, the frontier became increasingly more vulnerable to Comanche and Apache attacks.

Homesteads were left to the protection of whoever was left to fire a weapon. Young men that could be spared from their homesteads eagerly sought to join the Texas Cavalry for the Confederate cause. Cole was old enough, but declined. Their homestead sat directly in the path of old Comanche war trails and now and then some newly empowered "leader" of the Comanche would try his luck against the small Stockton homestead.

One after the other Comanche attackers died. Their dead and broken bodies were buried in one of two cemeteries on the ranch. Flint Stockton insisted that every man had a soul. For that thought, the Stockton family would dress up a mite and stand over the burial of those that they killed. Flint read the Bible over their burying. There was no score kept, but it was generally acknowledged that Cole had a pretty fair hand in adding to the count.

CHAPTER EIGHT

The Scavengers

During the Civil War, scavengers—deserters, from both sides of the war, rode in groups or gangs and took everything in their wake. Some of them fanned out to the West Texas area. One of these gangs rode into the area of the Stockton Range on an early summer day.

The Mason gang numbered about twenty-five men, all of them rough and rugged. They were no strangers to rifle, pistol, or knife. They lived off spoils of the land. What they wanted, they took, and the deadly toll from their hands numbered high.

At high noon the sun was unmerciful in its heat. Dust devils whirled across the plains and shimmering heat waves danced before red-rimmed eyes. It was during such a day that ten members of the Mason gang, an advance group, rode slowly onto the Stockton spread and fanned out like they normally did. There appeared to be no one in the yard.

Whit Jenson, leader of the scouting group, sat his horse in front of the house for a long moment, taking mental note of the ranch's physical assets. He thought, "We'll do well taking from this spread." He rose in his stirrups and called out to the seemingly empty house in a loud booming voice, "You there! You in the house! Come out and face us!"

The door slowly opened and a tall, lanky man in his forties stepped out to the stone porch. Jenson immediately took in the manner in which the man wore his gun. It sat comfortably on his right hip. The man was also carrying a rifle.

Jenson's grin curled up in a calculating manner. He and his men could easily gun down this man in a hailstorm of bullets.

"What can I do for you?" asked Flint Stockton.

"We're here to take whatever we want. You'll stand aside, or we'll shoot you down and take everything anyway."

"Thought as much. Cole! Clay! Step on out here. Johanna, you got that shotgun ready?"

"Yes, Flint. I've got him right in my sights."

Two younger men stepped out to the stone porch to stand with their father. Both were well armed with revolvers and rifles.

Whit Jenson swallowed hard. He knew that at least a shotgun was trained on him and now the taller of the two younger men standing in front of him wore that Colt Army revolver like he knew how to use it. Jenson looked into the young man's eyes and he saw the quick flash of his own death. A sudden shiver ran down his back and he had the feeling in the back of his mind that he was facing the eternal fires of hell.

"I've got some advice for you, scavenger," stated Flint Stockton. "Ride out and don't ever come back. You come back, we'll bury you over there with the rest of them that had the same ideas."

Jenson turned slowly and looked where Flint Stockton was pointing. There looked to be about twenty graves. He swallowed hard. He was no fool. He and his ten men could shoot, that was true, but he also knew that if anything started at this moment, he was a dead man.

Jenson turned slightly in the saddle and told his men to ride out. "They've got us covered Boys. Let's ride out." And under his breath he muttered the line "for the time being."

In the back of Jenson's mind was the notion that if Mason agreed, they would come back quietly at night. Then *all* would be theirs. The ranch, the spoils, and the woman would all would be theirs for the taking.

Jenson and his riders left the Stockton ranch and rode hard to their main camp where he told his leader of the small ranch and of the caliber of its defenders.

Frank Mason listened intently, and his face grew ugly mean. "You let a family of four homesteaders buffalo you? Hell, Whit, homesteaders ain't gunmen. We've proved that over and over. We, all of us, are going back there tonight and we are going to take that homestead and burn it to the ground. I want to see the nester family that can take all twenty-five of us. We'll kill all present, except for the woman and then we'll all have her as well as the spoils. Get some sleep. It's going to be a long night."

At the same time, Johanna Stockton turned to her husband, Flint, after the outlaw group rode out toward the northwest. "Flint. You know that they are coming back, don't you?"

"Yes, Dear. I highly suspect that they will be back here tonight and try to burn us out. Let's plan a surprise for them. Cole, you and Clay go and dig up that cache of powder that we buried behind the barn. Johanna, get a hot fire going in the fireplace. We have some lead to melt down into bullets."

Johanna turned to face Flint. "I sure wish that Jasper was still around. We could use an extra gun hand."

"Yah, but Jasper's gone to New Mexico Territory and we're here. Don't worry Johanna. We've done it before, and we'll do it again. This here is our land and it seems that if we want to keep it, we'll have to fight for it."

"It was just a thought, Flint."

"I know, Johanna. I wish that Jasper was here also. He was my best friend—still is. I sure wish that he would write and let us know what he is doing."

Their conversation was suddenly interrupted by both of their sons entering the house with two kegs of black powder.

Cole spoke first. "Here they are, Pa. What do you want us to do with them?"

"We are going to make a lot of bullets, we may need them. Secondly, let's cut up about five large squares of cloth and get some very long fuses. We are going to place some homemade explosives at just the right spots all around the yard. We're going to have some real fireworks tonight."

*　　　*　　　*

Close to midnight the band of twenty-five scavengers approached the Stockton ranch. They had planned the raid with care and, tonight, that homesteader family was going to have the surprise of their lives.

Whit Jenson rode to the left with ten riders. Frank Mason rode to the right with ten riders. Five others rode toward the dark shadows of the barn and corrals. The five would take the barn and keep hot firing straight into the house while the others would ride up from the sides and throw burning brands onto the roof. When the house burned brightly, those homesteaders would have no choice but to run out into the gunfire of the outlaws and then, all would be theirs.

The selected five men rode quietly to the back of the barn and dismounted. They found the door unlatched and, grinning to each other, entered the darkened building. They found a coal lamp and struck a match. Even as the match flared up, they heard an unmistakable "click" of metal sliding against metal from the shadows.

All five men looked toward the sound and found that they faced a lanky young man of perhaps eighteen years. He had the unmistakable mischievous grin on his face that resembled a small boy caught raiding a cookie jar.

"Howdy, scavengers. Drop your guns or take lead."

"Five against one, Boy. We're going to fill you with lead and walk right over your dead carcass."

There were no second words from Cole Stockton. He simply shot the man on the left in the stomach, the next man to him in the chest, and then flung himself to the dirt floor of the barn. He rolled to the left, straight into a stall. The three remaining raiders also dived into stalls while drawing their weapons.

Inside the darkened house, three figures waited with guns at the ready. Several shots cracked from the barn. "They're here," remarked Flint, "Watch the shadows carefully."

A match flared to the right and Johanna squeezed off a shot directly at it. A scream followed. Johanna smiled. "One more down. I hope Cole is all right."

"Don't even think about it, Johanna. Cole will take care of himself. We need to take care of those coming at us."

Several matches flared up and brands were fired. Fast moving figures were outlined as the burning torches moved steadily toward the house.

"Make every shot count!" yelled Flint as he lined up on his first target.

A gang member, Warren Jackson, was riding hard to the left of the Stockton house, a burning brand in his right hand. He was going to throw it onto the roof. His arm was cocked almost to the throwing point when the heavy caliber lead drove through his chest and exited his back. The hot burn severed his spine and he slipped like jelly from his horse to land hard on the ground. He felt nothing. He couldn't move anything. He just lay there dying with unbelieving eyes.

Clay Stockton reloaded the heavy Sharps rifle and lined up for another target.

Another raider drove straight toward the house firing his revolver in his left hand and carrying a burning torch in his right. He was twenty yards from the house when the full blast of a shotgun tore into his body and he jerked out of the saddle to slam lifelessly onto the ground. The burning brand fell on top of him and set fire to his clothes.

Frank Mason swore, "Damn them homesteaders! They was waiting for us! All of us at the same time—rush them and burn them out!"

The three remaining raiders in the barn had their hands full. They had dived into opposite stalls and were stuck. Two of their gang lay sprawled dead in the middle of the aisle and to jump and run would be suicide. That kid held a line on the center row of the barn and anyone moving into it, especially to make for the door could be shot down in an instant.

"Give you one more chance before I have to kill all of you. Throw your guns to the center row. Stand up and step out with your hands held high."

One raider motioned to the others. "Throw one gun out and put the other in your belt behind your back. When we step back for him to get our guns, we draw our belt guns and kill him."

The men did as ordered, throwing guns out to the center aisle and stepping into it with hands raised.

Cole Stockton did not step into the aisle way right a-way as they had thought. He eased his Colt revolver around the corner of the stall, pointing it directly at the leader's middle. The leader heard the click of metal and then knew that if anyone moved—he was a dead man.

At the front of the house, Whit Jenson and Frank Logan screamed at their men, "Let's go! Kill them all!"

They rode forward, meeting a hail of gunfire from the house and from the barn. It suddenly dawned on Frank Logan that all five of his men in the barn had been either taken or shot dead.

Jenson rode hard to the front of the house, firing into the house as fast as he could. In one instant, he was rushing forward and shooting his revolver, in the next instant, his body was flying through the air with a sudden blast of light, that Jenson didn't recognize as a bomb, his body was picked up from his horse and thrown high into the air. He landed with a thud, the wind knocked out of him. He tried to move and found that both legs were broken, his left arm was disjointed. He felt warm blood flowing and, putting his hand to his face, found that he no longer had a nose. He had ridden directly into the center of an explosion.

Several more explosions went off at various sectors of the property, and Jenson saw more men fly through the air just like him. Their powder-burned and broken bodies slammed to earth—unmoving.

Amid the screams of dying men and horses, Frank Mason quickly surveyed the situation and with two other henchmen, pulled back on the reins, turned their horses toward the West and sunk spur.

They had gone only a quarter of a mile when a loud boom shattered the din of travel. One raider pitched backward off of his horse with a large caliber bullet in his chest.

"Ya'll be running from the Stockton homestead, I reckon. Draw in them ponies or die where you sit."

Mason and his remaining partner reined in as ordered, raising hands high above their heads.

A man rode out from behind a clump of mesquite trees and approached them. He was an older man, riding tall and lean, his dark eyes gleamed with a sense of honor and justice. There was a no-nonsense look on his face and he held the Springfield rifle pointed directly at them.

"Just came to visit friends and I find ya'll raiding their home and trying to kill them. Now, that ain't nice. Let's turn around and rejoin the party. Make a false move and I will have to fill your ugly carcasses with lead."

The Stockton family had counted the dead and lined up the few wounded and captured raiders when mounted dark shadows entered the yard. Two of the riders held their hands up high. The third man was behind them and seemed to be controlling them with commands.

Johanna immediately recognized the voice. "Jasper Rollins!"

"Howdy, Johanna. I caught these skunks trying to run. What say we hang them on the spot? That's what we would have done in the old days, huh, Flint? I can make a noose just so. Do you want to strangle these two, or merely break their necks on the fall?"

Frank Mason could just about feel the noose tightening around his neck as he thought about Jasper Rollins' words.

Flint Stockton spoke up. "Jasper! It's good to see you again. Thanks for the help. I think that we ought to let the punishment fit the crime. They wanted to burn us out. Let's burn them like the Apache would. Stretch out their bodies over the white hot coals of a fire. Or, we could just tie them up to the corral bars and shoot hell out of them—like targets."

"Now, that's a dandy idea, Flint. Besides, I'm feeling old and cranky and I need a bit of diversion. Yes. Targets will do."

Frank Mason looked fervently around the yard. Besides him and the man with him, only five of their men survived the attack, and now, it seemed that they were about to be executed. Jasper and the Stockton family lined all of the scavengers along the corral fence. The raiders stood shaking against the corral bars as all the members of the Stockton family and Jasper Rollins took careful aim at them and pulled their triggers.

All five bullets smacked into the railings all around them. One man fainted with fright. Frank Mason's eyes went wide and crazy. He had stared straight into the eyes of a young Cole Stockton and saw his own soul burning in the fires of Hell.

The frightened men were removed from the corral bars, led into the barn and locked up in the tack room until they could be transported to the local law.

Flint turned to his long time friend, "Jasper, what brings you back here to Texas?"

"Well, Flint. I found a range of many, many wild horses. I thought that I might come back here and pick up Cole and together we might form sort of a partnership. He's young and can work the horses. I can sort of find them, cook, clean up camp, build us a cabin to live in and talk him through some things. I shore would like to have Cole with me."

Flint and Johanna Stockton looked toward their eldest son. He was eighteen now and needed to experience life on his own.

Silent consent passed between Flint and Johanna. A young Cole Stockton would go with Jasper Rollins to the New Mexico Territory and seek his destiny.

Two days after turning the surviving scavengers over to a detachment of the Frontier Battalion of Rangers, Cole Stockton along with Jasper Rollins said their farewells to Johanna, Flint, and Clay, and rode side by side toward the setting sun. New Mexico Territory beckoned in the distance and Cole felt the wonder in his heart. He was now on his own and was to experience whatever life brought him. He was ready and willing, and he had a good friend and trusted teacher at his side.

Jasper grinned at him, "Are you ready for this?"

"Yes, Jasper. I think that I am ready to be on my own."

"Yah, Cole. I think that you are. Look out world. Here comes Cole Stockton and Jasper Rollins!"

CHAPTER NINE

Jasper and Me

I was well into my eighteenth year when ole retired Texas Ranger, Jasper Rollins, invited me to partner with him and hunt wild horses in the New Mexico Territory. At the time, good saddle-broke horses would bring fair money to those that braved the wilds, the elements, and the perils of marauding Indians, rustlers, and other hard men who made their living by taking from other hapless folks. Then too, were the hardships of several months to find, trap, break to saddle, and sell these horses. Nevertheless, we were of a mind to do just that.

We looked quite the pair. Jasper was in his late fifties or so. He stood six foot one, and slender, with hard muscles that were likened to steel springs. He had a weathered face highlighted by slightly grayish hair and dark piercing eyes. On the other hand, I was the proverbial skinny kid with light sandy colored hair and blue-green eyes. Well, I guess that I could say that although skinny, I was tall and wiry.

That the two of us were gun savvy was evidenced by the manner in which we wore the Colt revolvers strapped to our waists. Both of us carried a Bowie knife behind our left hip as well as a Henry repeating rifle slung in a saddle scabbard. To some, it would seem that we were loaded for bear. But, that was the way of it in those days. A man had to fend for himself as there was no law to speak of and there were plenty that fancied themselves able to take what you worked hard to build for yourself.

Jasper had an eye for the landscape and when we neared the New Mexico Territory, he advised me in his usual manner of very few words. "We're there now," he said softly. "We'll be where we ought to be in another day or so." And, thus began my continued education of the hard land, hard men, and the elements of nature.

It seemed like we rode for a good four to five days before coming across any semblance of civilization. I don't recall the place as even having a name. It was just a few adobe buildings set within the vicinity of several watering springs. I took stock of the location and thought it a good place to water a lot of cattle.

Anyways, Jasper and I climbed down off our horses and stretched a bit. I remember feeling stiffer than ever before. That was probably because I'd never taken such a long ride before this. Well, we led off to what seemed a central corral for passing folks to water, feed, and rest their mounts.

After caring for our stock, Jasper and I drew our rifles from the saddle scabbards and walked over toward a cantina. Well, what can I say? It was the only place that advertised food as well as "spirits" and beer.

Just as we approached the door, Jasper turned to me and said, "Cole, I don't reckon that you've ever been in a place like this, so, let me give you a few quick insights before we walk in. Firstly, there are rough men in there. Some are very apt to be quite rowdy and want to fight with someone. We're here for a meal and to rest a bit only. After that, we'll go on down the trail and find us a good secluded campsite. We don't tell anyone the why's and wherefore's of why we're here. O.K., follow my lead."

We entered the dimly lit atmosphere. After stepping a bit to the right and left of the door, our eyes took only a moment to accustom ourselves to the dimness of the room. About nine rough-looking men stood at the makeshift bar speaking in low tones and partaking of various spirits of whiskey, tequila, and beer. A dozen or so others sat around tables playing cards and drinking likewise. I appeared to be the youngest one there.

Jasper motioned me to a table in a corner and sauntered up to the bar. He spoke softly to the unkempt looking Mexican bartender.

"Comida. Food, for me and my friend over there," and he motioned with a nod of his head toward me.

The bartender nodded and called out a quick phrase in Spanish. Momentarily, a young woman of about my age emerged from a hallway door and brought us an earthen jug of water with two tin cups. She smiled widely at me with appraising eyes. I smiled back.

She brought us tortillas, spiced beef, frijoles (refried beans), and a spicy rice mixture for a nominal price, and Jasper ordered us both a beer.

It didn't take long until we were partaking of this grub. I found it quite tasty. Once again the girl stopped back at our table and asked in her broken English, if we needed anything else. Jasper reached into his pocket and placed the cost of our meal and just a little bit more on the table, then pushed it toward her. She nodded and said, "Gracias, Senors. I am Elena. Should you come back here, I would be pleased to serve you."

We had just stood up and made ready to walk out the door when three men entered the cantina. They, like us, had stopped briefly in the dimness, for their eyes to adjust.

Suddenly, they looked at Jasper and jerked wide-awake. They moved to the side and spread out, hands nervously wavering near their guns. Jasper grinned a bit and announced, "Well, well, iffen it ain't Abraham Martin and his two boys, Jerald and Isaac. It's been a long time, Abe. But, I ain't looking for y'all anymore. I've retired from the Rangers. You can do as you please."

Abraham glared at Jasper and sort of growled, "I ain't forgetting Zeke, Jacob, and Jeremiah. You killed all three of them and they's kinfolk. You mark my words, Jasper Rollins, they will be avenged."

Jasper replied, "Well, Abe. They were just plain dumb, slow witted, and refused to give up. I always thought you had more sense, but I see the relationship now. Why don't we just settle this here and now? Your hand is close to that hogleg, PULL IT! Let's end it here once and for all."

Bystanders in the cantina quickly moved to the walls and end of the bar, well out of the line of fire, anticipating momentary deadly action to start between our two factions.

Abe clenched his teeth with an evil look in his eyes. "Not now, Jasper. Not here! I want you in my time. I want you in my grasp to wane out your soul and take you a little bit at a time. I am going to wear you down and when you are haggard and spent, Old Man, I am going to put a bullet right between your eyes. You are going to suffer for what you did to my brothers and cousin."

While Jasper was trading words with Abraham, I kept my eyes on the two younger ones. They both sort of stared daggers at me, sizing me up, I suppose. My wrist sat easy right at butt level to my Colt and I watched their eyes. They didn't seem to like it one bit. First thing was that they didn't know me. Secondly, they didn't like the way that my right hand sort've stayed right at my Colt.

Well, finally, they moved towards the bar and gave us a wide berth. One of the boys, Jerald, chuckled to me as we backed out of the door, "And, You! You are my MEAT! I'm taking you down too, whatever your name is."

I looked him straight in the eye and calmly said, "Name's Cole Stockton, and anytime you want to prance your pony, trot it on out."

Well, he didn't like that, but his pa kept him in check. That was when I got the evil eye from the Ole Man also. I knew then, that I was marked for death same as Jasper.

We backed out of the cantina, then turned and made our way back to the corrals for our mounts. Nothing was said between us as we put boot to stirrup and swung into the saddle. We turned out toward the west and trotted through the main street, such as it was. We needed to put a few miles between that bunch and us.

Once out of sight of the town, we turned northward and traveled for yet another hour. Dusk found us settled down within a ravine with a low fire. It may have been a scrawny rabbit on that spit, but it tasted good to us. We talked a bit, and Jasper related the story of his dealings with the Martin family: "The Martin's were well suited to bullying and taking from those less fortunate when they'd a mind to, and I caught up with the two brothers and cousin when they had stolen stock in hand, so to speak."

Jasper reflected a long moment before continuing, "Texas Ranger fashion at that time was to enact the full course of justice to those found guilty with the evidence or goods of the crime upon their persons, and I did my bound duty to the state of Texas by executing them on the spot. I did, however, knowing the family somewhat, show them the courtesy of carrying the demised back for deliverance to family resting places."

Jasper looked deep into my eyes and related further, "None of this set well with the Martins. They had one notion and only one notion, that being—I kilt one of their own and to that end, I was to be found and kilt myself, never mind that their kin was outlawed or even murderers and thieves."

My own thought was that the Martin family was bent on revenge and I saw that hatred glowing within their eyes as we backed out of that cantina back there.

The stars were twinkling brightly when we finally rolled into our blankets and sought out sleep. Night sounds were normal as we settled down and closed our eyes. The thing about nature is that when a man is used to traveling the wilds, he emanates various scents and accustoms himself to the elements. He becomes one with the earth.

We were akin to the sights and sounds of the night, the slight scurry of a tiny animal through the brush, the slight sigh of the wind, and yes, even the stillness of the air that signals peacefulness or danger.

*   *   *

We rose before first light and sensed rather than felt our way around our small camp. When the first ray of sunlight broke across the edge of the earth to the east, we were standing straight and surveying the land before us, and especially, the land behind us.

Jasper took a long moment to scan our back trail, and then he shook his head and softly drawled, "They're looking for us. See that slight glow to the south? That's a campfire, and sure as shooting it's them Martin's. They'll be out looking for our tracks directly. We need to find some rocky ground first—and then, we'll play a few ole Jasper tricks on them."

Jasper led off to the west as the early morning light changed obscure shapes and shadows into recognizable landscape. At the end of an hour, Jasper changed direction and we rode toward the north. We kept our eyes peeled for something out of the ordinary, like rocky ground, and finally in the next hour we entered a deep arroyo that led a winding path. It was just the ticket. We were below the visible landscape and couldn't be readily seen by anyone traveling parallel to us. We followed it for a few miles until it ran flush with the upper level. We changed direction again, bearing east for a few miles. The landscape changed with us and soon we were amongst rough and rocky terrain. We followed the incline to higher ground. When we reached what seemed to be the summit, Jasper signaled to dismount. We took a breather and quietly surveyed our back trail. Neither of us could detect any movement below us for miles.

"I think we done it. I think that we've lost them for a while Cole. But, mark my words, they'll be scouring the area for our sign."

We mounted and turned once again northward. Jasper knew exactly where we were headed. I wished that I did.

At noon, we made a cold stop. We rested the horses and sipped warm water from our canteens. Cold biscuits and beef jerky were the faire. Later in the evening, we would find a place to build a small fire for coffee and a hot meal. After that, the fire would be doused and we'd sit in the darkness and speak in low tones. Later, one of us would sleep and the other would stand watch. That was the way of it until we reached the place where we would set up our horse hunting operations.

The next morning, we once again struck out to the north. I noticed the obvious changes in the landscape. This land was ideal for wild horses to roam freely and hide from untrained eyes.

Mid-morning we came across the presence of numerous signs of wild horses. We found a few tracks, some droppings, and various paths forged through grassy areas. Every so often, our own mounts sniffed the air when slight breezes stirred the stillness. By the end of the day, we were in the area that Jasper had in mind for us. It was a beautiful somewhat hidden valley that teemed with long flowing grasses and a variety of trees. We rode to the far end of the valley noticing sign of wild horses everywhere.

The spot that Jasper had in mind was in a small box canyon of sorts. It had a small stream flowing leisurely past a woods. There was good grass for feed and there were trees and heavy brush enough to build a holding corral and a lean-to shack for our use. We dismounted, stripped our gear off the horses, and set about to make a comfortable camp. Rocks were gathered to form a fire pit and we cut saplings to form the framework of a crude shelter. The stripped off branches were woven into mats that we tied together for a makeshift roof of sorts.

One of life's small pleasures is a good cup of coffee. Jasper's brew tasted especially good that evening. We finally got a hot meal of potatoes, beans, and bacon. After supper, Jasper rolled himself a smoke and we lay around speaking of the days to come.

"Cole, in the morning we will begin to seal off areas of this canyon so our captive horses can't escape. Then, we will form a working corral to work our horses one at a time. I believe that we should fashion some long bars—about three should do. They will serve as a gate to the entrance of this canyon. Once we've settled our working area, we'll ride around the valley to get our bearings. We'll take note of any horse signs and plot it out. We'll find horses and bring them to this spot, and then after we get about a dozen or so, we'll break them to saddle. They'll be easier to handle that way. When we get about a hundred head, we'll move them to Taos, about two days ride northeast from here. We'll find a market for them there."

"Jasper, I've heard of Taos, New Mexico Territory, from travelers and plainsmen that passed through our homestead from time to time. Father always welcomed them and their stories of what they saw and experienced. That was the way we learned news in our neck of the woods."

Jasper chuckled a bit at my remarks, then continued, "Within a few months we should have some good spending money. Always remember, Cole, that when the chips are down and things seem to go against you, go and find a few horses and break them to saddle. You will never go hungry that way."

I acknowledged Jasper's wisdom with a nod and silly grin. I'd already heard that same piece of advice from my father on more than one occasion.

Jasper finished his smoke and we let the fire die down to simmering coals. We lay back against our saddles and rolled up in our blankets. This was the first time that we'd both slept at the same time in quite a while.

*   *   *

The morning came softly as I woke to the smell of bacon frying. Jasper was his usual self, waking with first light and working his morning chores.

"Morning," he drawled softly, "Got some breakfast ready. Once we've eaten, we'll set to working on our holding area."

A little over three days later, Jasper and I had built a makeshift fence across the creek to keep our wild horses from escaping through the stream. We gathered large amounts of heavy brush and set them entangled to form a wall across the entrance of the canyon. We fashioned three long bars from small trees and set them into a lashed post framework to serve as a gate to our site. Towards sunset on the third day, we looked back over our work and felt satisfied that we were ready to begin the hunt. We would start in the morning.

Jasper rustled us up a pot of fresh coffee along with a supper of potatoes, dried beef, beans and a few wild scallions that I had found in a grassy area of the canyon. While we were eating, Jasper mentioned that one of us would have to take the ride into Taos before long to get basic food supplies if we were to stay the hunt. Then Jasper got a real serious look to his face.

I looked across the campfire at him, my head cocked to one side with a quizzical expression.

"Cole, I like this valley and this canyon. When I first saw it I knew it was my place to be here. I feel at peace here, and here is where I want to be laid to rest when the Lord calls me. Promise me that should something happen, that you will carry out my wishes."

I looked deep into Jasper's eyes. He looked tired, and now I understood why he had wanted me along with him. He was giving me my first chance at the world, as well as to have someone along with him that he trusted with his wishes. I thought then, that perhaps Jasper had some sort of premonition. I let it go, not wishing to pursue my thought.

"Jasper, you've been a second father to me. You've taught me well in the matter of reading men and the land. I will do as you wish."

He nodded and then with a heavy sigh, spoke softly, "Let's turn in Cole. There's a lot of tracking to do with first light."

*   *   *

I reckon that it was sometime after midnight when I sensed the mist and eased up from my blankets. There was definitely moisture in the air and within the next few minutes, it started to rain, first with sprinkles and then in a slow drizzle. No lightning flashed nor thunder rumbled. It was a peaceful, slow, life giving rain. I thought then, we wouldn't get much horse hunting done if it was still raining by full light. I turned over and pulling the blankets up around my neck for warmth, and slipped back into sleep.

Morning came and the rain stopped. The ground was damp and muddy in places. When I looked at the creek bed, I saw it had risen some. I looked over at Jasper and found him watching the sky.

"It will be clearing soon. Not good ground-wise to try to catch horses, but good enough to scout the valley for signs and to plot our findings. We'll start directly after coffee and biscuits."

A half hour later we were in the saddle, riding the edge of the valley. Our eyes swept the landscape as we rode slowly, constantly watching for wild horse sign.

Jasper was slightly ahead of me when he reined his horse, Sonnet, to a halt. I stopped also and watched Jasper. He stared at the ground for a long time, and then he searched the horizon in a round-a-bout fashion.

Within a moment, he motioned me to side him. I moved alongside and saw the concerned look on his face. Jasper pointed to the ground before us. There were tracks, but not just any tracks—they were unshod pony tracks and it wasn't just one pony. There were several.

"We're not alone Cole, there's others in the valley. We are going to have to find them, and see who they are."

Jasper drew his Henry rifle and led out following the tracks. I was right beside him, my rifle also at the ready.

We followed the tracks all the way to the end of the valley but found no one. The tracks continued out of the valley and veered south. Jasper reckoned on that. "Cole," he said to me, "Let's hope that they keep on moving. By the direction they're headed, they might be Apache, and that's bad news in anyone's language."

We turned and continued our wild horse tracking, the ever present thought in the back of our minds that we would have to be ever vigilant in our work.

Within the week Jasper and I had found and corralled our first dozen wild horses and I began working them into saddle stock with Jasper's assistance. It seemed that he took great pleasure watching me "riding high" on each horse. I caught a quick glimpse of him grinning widely each time that I mounted one, got thrown off, got up, dusted myself off to climb back into the saddle. Soon, the first three horses were broken to saddle. My disposition and my body were sore and aching by nightfall but I was getting the hang of it. Jasper rubbed some liniment into my sore back and shoulders as he praised the job that I was doing.

"You're doing good, Cole. A horse or so a day should be a good schedule. Tomorrow, I'll go to Taos for supplies. You'll stay here and work the rest of the horses to saddle. Now, don't you go a hunting any more horses until I get back. Just stay put right here in camp. Don't even go out of the canyon. A man that moves leaves tracks and we don't want to leave too many right now. I should be back within three or four days with enough grub and such to last a good while."

The next morning Jasper saddled up Sonnet while I rigged the packhorse with its packsaddle and gear. Once done, he pulled his list from a shirt pocket to go over it again. When he was satisfied that we'd noted all that we needed in supplies, he again cautioned me to stay within our camp.

"I will stay", I replied.

Jasper shook hands with me, and then swung up into the saddle. I opened our makeshift corral gate for him as he led out of the canyon entrance. He turned slightly in the saddle and gave a farewell wave. Moments later, he was on his way to Taos. I sighed and looked to the next horse that I would work to saddle.

CHAPTER TEN

Dark Premonitions

Jasper Rollins rode warily through the valley with packhorse in tow. His eyes constantly swept the terrain around him, ever vigilant for sign that he was not alone. After clearing the edge of the valley and moving into an area of vast rolling prairie dotted with clumps of grasses, mesquite, and sage brush; he found tracks of a group of pronghorn antelope. They were moving in the same direction as he.

Jasper followed the path of the antelope for an hour or so, then he noticed that their tracks seem to suddenly move to the right and then left of the direction they had been going. He thought, "Something must've startled them. I wonder what it was."

His question was answered within fifty yards of the skittering animal tracks. There he found more tracks—human tracks, moccasin tracks to be exact, and they were moving to the left of Jasper. There appeared to be at least three Indians by the looks of the trail.

Jasper sat Sonnet for a long minute while he pondered his next move. Sweat beads formed on his brow and trickled down his bewhiskered, weather beaten face. He decided that the tracks probably belonged to a hunting party and he elected to continue his trek to Taos, keeping a good pace and a clear mind as to his surroundings. A short while later, he heard the bantering of some jaybirds and instinctively knew that all was well at the moment.

Jasper's travel continued to move onto higher ground. When he spied a good stand of trees along a rock formation in the distance, he decided to make a cold camp there for the night. His fare would be jerky and water from his canteen for no fire would be lit to show his position.

Jasper stripped Sonnet and the packhorse of their trappings and after picketing the packer, he let them feed on the tall grasses around the campsite. Then, he put out his bedroll at the base of a tree and laid back silently recalling the travel of the day past and of the journey ahead. Sometime around midnight Jasper slipped into a light sleep, Colt revolver close to hand, and mindful of the night sounds that were supposed to be there.

*   *   *

The early grey of morning found Jasper saddling up Sonnet and outfitting the packhorse. Before mounting and leading out of the campsite, he moved to the edge of the rock formation to scan his back trail and the surrounding area. He saw no movement other than a couple of hawks gliding high on air currents. He watched them briefly and satisfied that all was well, swung up into the saddle and led out of the trees toward his destination.

The remaining journey to Taos was uneventful. Jasper entered the town in the late afternoon. He sought out the livery stable for his animals and found it just off of the town square. He arranged for feed and water for each horse as well as a place in the loft for himself to lay his head for the night. Then, taking his Henry rifle and saddle bags, he strolled down to the main plaza searching for the general store where he would purchase his supplies.

Entering the general store, Jasper found the storekeeper and stood patiently nearby while the man waited on two women. Jasper scanned the stock of goods displayed on the shelves as well as items stacked neatly on tables and counters. The store was well stocked with tins of fruit and vegetables, as well as sacks of coffee, flour, sugar, and corn meal. There were barrels of salt pork, bacon, apples, dried beans, and crackers. Dry goods, such as materials, blankets, and some clothing were stacked on a back counter. Jasper took in the gun racks and ammunition stock as well.

When the storekeeper finished with the female customers Jasper stepped up to the counter, producing his list. "I'd like for you to fill this order and have it ready first thing in the morning. I'll bring my packhorse around to the front of the store right about daybreak. Can you do that?"

The bespectacled, apron clad, storekeeper read down the list. With a pleasant smile, he acknowledged that he would have Jasper's order ready with the first light of day. As a second thought, Jasper pointed to the ammunition shelves, "Add about four boxes of .44 caliber to that list. I might be needing them." The man nodded his understanding.

Jasper left the general store and strolled out into the plaza. The man was hungry for some local southwestern flavor. He glanced around the plaza and spotted a cantina. "They've probably got some good vittles in there," he thought.

The old Ranger made his way through the early evening crowd of locals and a variety of visitors. Many were Indians and people of Spanish descent packing up their wares from the day's market. Some Anglos stood around the Plaza talking while smoking home rolled cigarettes. Within the hour, the vendors would be gone home.

Jasper stepped through the batwing doors into the cantina and then waited a moment, allowing his eyes adjust to the dimness. The dank air inside was similar to most saloons Jasper had previously visited, laced with the unmistakable hint of stale beer and tobacco smoke. He made his way to the bar and met a stocky Spanish bartender. Jasper ordered up a beer and asked about a meal. The bartender motioned to a table toward the back of the cantina where a doorway outlined a small kitchen. Other men sat at tables in that area with plates of food. Jasper nodded, then moved to a table along the back wall.

Within a few moments of seating himself, a young Spanish girl of perhaps fourteen appeared beside him. "Senor? What food for you this evening?" Jasper smiled at her then said "Enchiladas, por favor." She replied, "Si Senor, con arroz, frijoles y tortilla?" Jasper chuckled a bit and replied, "Si, Senorita. Muchas gracias." The girl smiled at Jasper and retreated to the kitchen. Jasper sipped on his beer and amused himself by examining the clientele. There were cowboys, a storekeeper or two, and those that appeared to be like himself, drifters. Jasper recognized no one.

Momentarily, the young girl appeared with Jasper's supper. He paid her a few pesos and motioned with his hand that she should keep any change for herself. Her eyes showed appreciation for the obvious tip that he had given.

Jasper finished his meal and rolled himself a smoke. He leaned back in the wooden chair and relaxed. He thought of the trip ahead in the morning and of young Cole Stockton who was working their horses in the canyon. He would return as fast as he could. Suddenly, a cold chill ran up Jasper's spine and he shuddered a bit. He took it as a foreboding sign, and sensed that he would face danger on this return trip. He thought, "I've had premonitions before, but not like this. I'll have to be very careful on the trail."

Jasper rose from the chair and made his way out to the plaza. Evening had come and those establishments still doing business, the hotels and cantinas, already had lanterns hanging lit outside their doors. He made his way to the livery stable for a night's rest. He saw to his animals and then climbed up the ladder to the loft. Jasper arranged a comfortable spot near some hay bales, then lay back, closed his eyes, and drifted into a soft slumber.

*   *   *

Early morning found Jasper Rollins tying up at the hitching rack at Canby's General Store. He took the packs off the packsaddle and carried them inside. Mr. Canby stood behind the counter waiting for him. He pointed to the end of the counter where he had packaged and stacked Jaspers order. "Good morning, sir. I have your supplies already packaged for you. Please go over the list with me and we'll make sure that all is there." Jasper listened while the storekeeper went down this list and then assured him that all was as he wanted. He paid the storekeeper in silver coins, which the man eagerly accepted.

Jasper waved farewell and left the store. He placed the packs on the packhorse and covered them with a tarp which he tied in place with a rope. Then, he mounted Sonnet and taking up the pack animal's lead rope, started across the Plaza. He rode out of town toward the West.

*   *   *

Unknown to Jasper, evil lurked within the shadows of an alleyway. Issac Martin relieved himself against the wall of a cantina and turned back toward the street just in time to see Jasper Rollins ride past the cantina. Issac scrambled to the street and ran excitedly into the cantina calling out, "Pa! Jerald!, I just seen Jasper Rollins there in the street. He's riding out of town."

Abraham Martin jumped up from his chair in the cantina, rushed to the batwing doors, and looked down the street where Issac pointed. He saw the man that they attempted to follow and kill, but lost track of over rocky ground. Now, Jasper was within their grasp once again. This time, they would not miss him. Abraham yelled at his boys, "Get the horses and meet me at the general store. I'm going to get some extra ammunition. We are going to track him down and I'm going to fill Jasper Rollins with hot lead before I cut out his heart and leave his body for wolves."

Issac and Jerald Martin bolted across the plaza to retrieve their horses and gear from the livery where they had left them the previous evening. Abraham entered Canby's General Store and stood anxiously at the ammunition counter while Canby waited on some other customers. After long minutes, Abraham announced in a loud voice that he was in a hurry and needed cartridges. Customers turned to look at him disapprovingly, but said nothing. The storekeeper, sensing trouble with this man, excused himself and moved to the guns and ammunition area of the store.

"Give me four boxes of .44's." growled Abraham as he slapped down silver coins on the counter, "and keep what's left for yourself, I'm in a hurry." He grabbed the cartridges and rushed through the store just as Issac and Jerald rode up with his horse in tow.

Mr. Canby watched with disgust as the three spurred their mounts out of town. He wondered would they have something to do with the man who bought four boxes of cartridges earlier. He shook his head as he went back to his other customers.

The Martins rode quickly down the dusty road west out of Taos. They couldn't see Jasper ahead of them, so the three men slowed to a steady walk and they looked for sign of two horses leaving the main road. They weren't the best trackers but they knew what they were looking for.

*   *   *

Jasper Rollins continued westward out of Taos toward his first goal, that being the same campsite where he rested at two days earlier. He remembered the commanding view of the terrain. That fact comforted him. He rode about four miles before turning in a southerly direction through tree lined slopes, zigzagging his way to level ground. Once, he skirted a clearing by riding around it, keeping his outline against the forest. Jasper continued to put distance ahead of those seeking his trail in deadly earnest.

Jasper's travel was uneventful the first day. Once in the rocky campsite, he unpacked his beast of burden and unsaddled Sonnet. He picketed the pack animal and then turned Sonnet out to feed on the tall grasses on the hill. The old man moved to the edge of the rocky ledge and surveyed his surroundings, taking special note of his back trail. Studying closely, he thought he caught a slight glint of fading sunlight on something shiny. He watched for a long time, and then, there it was again—a quick glimmer in the distance behind him.

The hair on the back of Jasper's neck bristled and the sense of danger once again seared across his brain. "There's someone out there, maybe following me. I'll cold camp tonight, no fire to point me out in the darkness. It will be very early when I leave here and I'll leave no trail."

Jasper ate jerky and drank water as the sun disappeared over the western horizon. Soon, all was pitch black except for the first stars of the night. The old man crawled to his vantage point again and searched the night for sign of possible adversaries. It wasn't long before his searching eyes located the reflection of dancing flames within a small campfire. Jasper noted the location and surmised that they were a few miles behind him. He thought, "Whoever it is, is camped for the night. They won't move until dawn and I'll be long gone."

*   *   *

It took Abraham Martin and his boys over an hour to find the place where Jasper Rollins left the main Taos road and moved into the forest. They followed his tracks and found his path of zigzag, daring not to divert from it. By nightfall, they still had not caught sight of Jasper. They decided to make camp with a low fire for coffee and a supper of beans and biscuits.

Abraham sat sullenly sipping his coffee and seething in the vengeance that would soon be his. "Sometime tomorrow boys, sometime tomorrow we will catch up with Rollins and I'll have my dues."

Jerald looked at his father across the campfire and a shudder ran up his spine. His father's eyes reflected the flames of the campfire and to him they looked like the fires of Hell itself. Once again he heard Abraham mutter "Vengeance is mine and it comes tomorrow."

Issac grinned as he toyed with his revolver in anticipation of emptying it into Jasper. He too would love it when they finally caught up with the old Ranger.

*   *   *

Dawn had not broken in the East as Jasper Rollins moved down the slope from his vantage point. He led out carefully, remembering every foot of the way to the lower sandy, brush covered terrain. From now on he meant to put miles between himself and those behind him.

As the sun rose, Jasper traveled quickly, stopping only every hour to rest his horses and wet their muzzles with water. He would keep that pace until within close range of the canyon and Cole Stockton. Still, he searched the horizon in front of him and also the trail behind him.

It was early afternoon. The sun was unmercifully hot. Jasper had almost reached the place where he had tracked the antelope on his way to Taos. He was watching the land in front of him when the crack of a rifle sounded behind him, and a bullet zipped past his head.

Jasper turned in the saddle, drawing his Colt revolver at the same time. He saw three horsemen fervently spurring their mounts toward him. He immediately surmised who they were and shouted to Sonnet, "HeHaw!, Sonnet, run. Come on packer, let's go!" The pack animal lunged into a run alongside Sonnet. Jasper fired a few rounds back at the Martins. He knew that he couldn't outrun them, but he had to find a place to make a stand. His eyes searched the now rolling mesquite covered plain for some semblance of cover. He saw what appeared to be ravine up ahead to the right and changed direction towards it. The Martins were rapidly closing the distance.

Just as Jasper reached the edge of the ravine, Sonnet stumbled, going down with a bullet in his heart. Jasper lunged headfirst to the ground and let go of the pack horse which went over the edge into the ravine. The packs slipped from his back and burst open. Supplies were strewn down the ravine as the pack animal escaped the crackling gunfire.

Jasper quickly jumped to Sonnet but saw that the horse was gone. He grabbed his Henry rifle and scrambled over the edge of the ravine to turn and line up on Jerald. He pulled the trigger and Jerald flung backward from the saddle, arms outstretched, hitting the ground without moving.

Abraham swore loudly as he rode to the left a ways before dismounting and crawling forward on the ground. He worked his way toward the ravine. Issac rode to the right and dismounted. He worked his way along the ground, pinning Jasper down to enable his father to get closer to him. Now Issac had another reason to kill Jasper. He had killed his brother.

At the edge of the ravine, Jasper searched for tell tale movement, but saw none. His eyes swept the area in front of him with blurred vision. He misted with tears for his horse, his companion, now dead at the hands of the Martins. He nodded silently. He would kill the remaining two men.

Issac moved forward slowly and deliberately until he was almost to the edge of the ravine. He hesitated briefly, cocked his revolver, and scrambled over the edge finding Jasper with his back to him. He fired twice as fast as he could. Jasper winced loudly from the first bullet and turned to face Issac. He fired into Issac's body just as the second bullet hit him in the side. Issac stumbled backward a step and Jasper shot him again in the chest. Issac jerked backward and hit the ground without moving.

Abraham dashed forward at the first crack of Issac's pistol and cleared the edge of the ravine just in time to see his youngest son slam to the ground. His eyes went wild with rage as he rushed at Jasper, firing his rifle wildly and missing the Ranger with each shot. Abraham emptied his rifle, then threw it to the ground. He drew his long knife from its scabbard and growled, "I'm gonna cut your heart out Rollins. I'm going to kill you dead!" He lunged at Jasper with the razor sharp blade.

Jasper, wounded but still game, dropped his rifle and rolled out of the way to come up with his own Bowie knife. Abraham turned with him, and lunged again. Jasper grabbed his wrist and the two men grappled for leverage. The elder Martin suddenly kicked Jasper in the knee. Jasper went down in searing pain, his side and back bleeding from the bullet wounds. Abraham moved in to kick Jasper again and again. He shouted loudly, "I'm gonna make you suffer Ranger! I'm gonna stomp you down and then, I'm gonna kill you!"

Jasper rolled away and somehow got to his feet. He wavered there holding his knife ready for the next attack. Abraham reached down and grabbed a handful of dirt, threw it into Jasper's face. Momentarily blinded by the dirt, Jasper swung his knife in an arch. He felt Abraham's knife slice into his chest and blood flowed freely. Jasper stumbled back and fell, losing the grip on his Bowie.

Abraham saw his chance and jumped onto Jasper. He grabbed his throat with one hand, choking him, and then, he raised his knife high in the air as he looked into Jasper's eyes. I'm going to cut out your living heart Rollins. I want to watch your face while I cut out your heart!"

Abraham Martin never saw the arrow that sunk deeply into his chest, but he was driven wide-eyed and backward from Jasper as it struck him. The last thing that Abraham saw was the three Mescalero Apaches standing around him and Jasper. His last words were, "The Apache will end your life for me. I'll see you in Hell, Rollins!"

Jasper coughed hard trying to regain his breath. He looked up into the dark eyes of the three Apache hunters and expected to die at any moment. He was greatly surprised, when one of the Apache spoke to him in broken English, "You are the tall horse hunter from the canyon. We watched the fight. You fought bravely. We will take you to your friend who tames the wild horses."

One of the Apache caught Jasper's pack animal. They rigged a drag from the tarp and helped Jasper onto it with care. They then took him to the entrance of the canyon. They called out loudly and then left silently, fading into the landscape.

Jasper lay on the makeshift drag aching from his wounds, knowing that the bullet in his back was mortal. Jasper thought "You never know about Apaches. You just never know what they will do."

*   *   *

I was sitting beside my small campfire thinking about Jasper. I had some dark premonitions during the night. I hoped that Jasper was alright. Suddenly, I heard a commotion at the entrance to the canyon. Somebody yelled loudly.

I grabbed up my Henry rifle and carefully worked my way to the makeshift brushy gate. At first I didn't see anyone. Presently, I heard some moans followed by my name, "Cole!, I need you. Come out here, son!" I moved forward and momentarily found Jasper bloodied and laying on that old tarp behind the pack horse which was tied to limbs of the gate. I moved quickly to his side. I looked into his pain filled eyes. I knew that I'd best get him inside to the fire. I untied the pack animal and led it to drag Jasper up to the campsite. There I lifted him off of the tarp onto a bed of blankets under the shelter of the lean-to. I pulled off his boots and made him as comfortable as I could. Jasper looked up into my eyes, attempted a smile of sorts, and then slipped off unconscious.

I heated water and used soap to bathe Jasper's wounds. I knew that he had lost a lot of blood. His wounds were bad. I dressed them as best as I knew how and then set to making broth from water and shaved beef jerky. I waited for Jasper to come around some so I could feed him the broth; he continued to sleep. I thought that rest would be best for him at this time.

It was near midnight when the soft drizzle of rain lightly drummed on the roof of the shelter. It continued until early morning. I had fallen asleep during the night, but rose before dawn to check on Jasper. I found him with a slight smile on his face and his eyes closed. Upon closer examination I knew that Jasper had passed on during the night or early morning.

I sat there for a long while, looking at this man I loved dearly, remembering all that he meant to me. He was a second father, a friend, and a teacher. Mist filled my eyes as I recalled Jasper's request. I had promised, and now, I would do as he bid me. I buried Jasper under a tree facing the creek and put wild flowers on his resting place. "He would like that," I thought.

I turned to go back to the campfire and was surprised to find three Apaches standing in front of me. One spoke in limited English. "Your friend was a great warrior. Be glad that his enemies are dead. They will hunt you no more. Go! Take those horses you have tamed and go. Do not come back here again." Before I could say anything they turned and were gone, fading like ghosts into the landscape.

I would do as they said. I would take my dozen horses to Taos to sell the lot. With what cash money I got from the sale, I would see the world on my own.

CHAPTER ELEVEN

Lessons from the Master

It was the summer of 1867, in northern New Mexico Territory, that I'd buried my long time friend and mentor, Jasper Rollins. Jasper had run into old adversaries and had a running fight with them. Some Apaches happened upon the fight and ended it. Jasper being mortally wounded, passed into the arms of his maker. I did for him the best that I could.

Apaches advised me to take my horses and leave that place, never to return. I did just that, and drove my remuda toward Taos. I was within a few miles of the settlement when I found an old run down ramshackle cabin with a dilapidated corral. I took it upon myself to move in and use it as a base of operations until I could find a buyer for my stock.

I then rode to Taos and inquired as to where I might sell a few horses broken to saddle. I was referred to the trading post and stagecoach operations just outside of the town. It was said that they paid fair money for good horseflesh, so I returned to the cabin, gathered up my stock and headed that way.

I was within a few miles of the nearest trading post and relay station when I happened upon three fellers coming my way. They appeared to be of dubious nature. They pulled up short and just sat on their animals looking over my stock and watching me herd my small remuda.

Them boys hailed me as I approached, and each had his own version of a crooked grin on his ugly face. I could see it coming as I read their minds, "three against one." Horses were easy money—especially if they weren't branded, like mine.

Well, they tried to ring me, and bully my animals from me. I turned my pony to one side, so they couldn't see my gun hand, and advised them to turn to and travel on.

Being older than I, and somewhat more experienced, they thought that they had easy pickings. All three reached for their irons at the same time.

My Colt Army .44 sort of leaped into my hand, and I was slinging hot lead as fast as I could thumb back the hammer and squeeze the trigger. I wasn't what you would call a real fast draw at that time, but I was somewhat of a dead shot, and as luck would have it, I shot and killed the first men since I was alone and on my own.

Not being one to shuck responsibility, I naturally tied the bodies over their saddles, and carried them to the stage station. I explained the situation to the stagecoach stationmaster, a tall thin man with gray hair and mustache called simply "Mac," who arranged for the burial. Looking over my stock, he offered to buy the whole lot. I found out later that his full name was Jack McCurdy.

"Well, son," he asked, "what do you call yourself?" as he handed me the money in gold coins.

"The name is—Cole. Cole Stockton," I answered.

"Cole," he said, "them boys likely got friends, and I would imagine that they will be a hunting you a'fore long. Would I were you, I would just take up a trail and go somewhere else. I would certainly hate to plant you beside them boys."

I knew one thing above all else. I couldn't run. I would have to face anything that came my way. That I was a *sure* shot was true, but, even a sure shot needs an edge. I bought extra ammunition at the trading post before heading back to my cabin.

After that, I took to practicing hard, after daily chores, to gain a smoother and quicker draw of my weapon. I took empty food tins and lined them up on the corral bar. Day after day of practice proved lethal to them cans. I got so's I could walk past them, turn—drawing as I did so, and nail all six cans in succession.

I guess those boys didn't have such good friends. A month passed, and no one showed up to claim a "notch." Around this time, I got a case of the wanderlust and decided it was time to move on. I'd been itching to see something of the Great Plains that I'd heard so much about, so I gathered up my possibles and lit a shuck for parts east.

The following months found me in the Kansas area, and that's when I first made the acquaintance of a gentleman there who made a lasting impression on me. Hays City was a mighty rough place, being near an army post and all. Gamblers, cowboys, homesteaders, soldiers, buffalo hunters, and ladies of the night filled the place. It seemed that nary a day passed that someone wasn't shot or robbed. Liquor flowed freely in the many saloons that vied for the off duty business of the newly formed 7th Cavalry troopers.

I had just settled my steel gray into a stall at the local livery and headed toward a hotel or boarding house for some much needed rest when I found myself in the immediate area of one burly gent who decided to have some fun. He shot the hat off an obvious city slicker and then fired at the slicker's feet in order to make him "dance." The dude's face was terror stricken as he jumped to and fro amidst showers of dirt plowed up by the gunman's bullets.

Ordinarily, I wouldn't have minded except nearby women and children cowered against storefronts along the street and I was afraid that his bullets would ricochet and hit some bystander. Well, I just sauntered up to within about fifteen feet of this gent, and told him so. I called for him to be careful.

He didn't take to my interfering with his fun and suddenly, he was looking straight at me with hard eyes—a look that sent chills to the bone. His wildly flashing eyes challenged me to make him. With attention turned to me, the city slicker saw his chance. He scooped up his hat from the ground and high tailed it down the street.

I guess that I stuck my foot into it again. "No need for anyone to get hurt," I calmly put it to him. That last statement riled him something fierce.

He holstered his pistol after a quick reloading, and verbally challenged me to draw against him. "I see that you're heeled. Well then, you young whelp, suppose you just show me how well you know that hogleg."

Pa always told me "Them that brag the most are more than likely to back off when put to the test." This one seemed to be an exception. He wasn't backing down, and I shore didn't figure him for having some friends to back him up, but, they were there—within the now gathering curious crowd, elbowing their way to the front.

They would've put me into a real tight situation had it not been for a tall, long-haired blonde gentleman wearing a frock coat, fancy vest, and two ivory handled Colt Navy .36's tucked in a red sash. He kind of stood to one side, and advised the gent's friends, "This is a one-to-one disagreement, and you will stay the hell out of it."

The ornery gent snarled out loud and boisterously for all to hear, "I don't need no help with a young whelp like this. Get ready to meet your maker, Sonny." His hand suddenly flashed for the revolver at his belt.

My own hand went to my Colt like it was born there, and I felt the iron rise smoothly out of the holster. Within the next instant, fire, smoke, and hot lead belched straight into that feller's middle, and he jerked with the impact. One hand instinctively covered the wound but his pistol was still rising into line with me when I shot him again. This time, his arms went askew and he slammed straight backward to the ground—dead.

His friends were stunned. It was easy to see by their unbelieving expressions that they had fully expected me to be lying there on the ground instead of their compadre.

James Butler Hickok, otherwise known as "Wild Bill," that tall blonde gentleman, looked me straight in the eye and nodded with a slight knowing smile on his otherwise sturdy expression.

Afterward, when the crowd had dispersed, the dead man had been carried off by the undertaker, and the local sheriff learned that the "dead one" drew first, "Wild Bill" asked me to join him for supper at a nearby café. I eagerly accepted his invitation because I was hungry, for one. Secondly, Hickok was a noted person and I valued any words of wisdom that he wished to impart.

We sat towards the back of the café, his back to the wall, and we made polite conversation. Then the conversation turned serious.

"That was a fool thing to do." he suddenly admonished, "Always watch for the second adversary, especially if the man is bragging loud.

They will always be there. Otherwise, you are a fair hand with that iron."

I reflected on that and freely admitted that I was somewhat inexperienced at that task commonly referred to as gun fighting. I also let it be known that I could probably use a good teacher.

Hickok looked deeply into my eyes as he asked the critical question. "Now, just why would you want to become a pistolero? It is dangerous business and not for the foolhardy. Once proven, you ride a lonely trail, devoid of normality, and have to stay forever vigilant for those eager to take your life."

I answered him the only way I knew how, by looking directly into those clear blue eyes and responding, "I've been in a few shooting scrapes already and need to defend myself. I honestly want to be the best that I can."

Hickok studied me for a long moment before replying, "I can understand that. All right, we'll start at daybreak tomorrow. Meet me out back of the livery."

Thus it began. I committed to learn the ways of the "gunman" from a man considered to be the master gunfighter.

Hickok taught me several tricks of the trade, to include the border shift, a technique used to switch hands while still shooting. He stressed keeping the hammer on an empty chamber unless six are needed, and always having a rifle with the same ammunition as my revolver. He advised me to never show more than one gun—unless you need two, and are good with both of them, including shooting with either hand.

Most importantly, he taught me to watch a man's eyes—watch for that quick little glint that precedes his hand reaching for his gun. He re-cautioned about multiple targets, and last but not least, "Expect to take lead. Steel your mind, Cole. Steel it against the pain that you will endure. Always remember this, any man who walks into a gun fight and expects not to get shot is a dead man."

That last sentence from Hickok was one I would always remember. Looking back over the years, I guess that it was that one thought, one bit of advice, that saved me from being out and out shot dead on many occasions. Once a man has shot another, euphoria rushes to his mind and he thinks, "I've done it. He's shot and dead."

Imagine the eyes of a would-be killer when you take the hit and recoil with it, turning with your Colt aimed straight at him somewhat like a duelist—and pull the trigger. The surprise is overwhelming, and lethal. Especially, if you have "fire" in your eyes and soul—an ever-consuming fire fueled by the desire to live.

His lessons also included, "When outnumbered, make every shot count. Most are anxious to get a faster draw—making the mistake of not aiming correctly." Hickok taught me that when staring at that pistol pointed at you—take careful aim and shoot the man dead. That lesson, I carried with me always, too. Other lessons I learned for myself as the next few years wore on.

Several times, the lessons that I learned from Hickok's hand proved paramount to my own survival. I became skilled at reading the "lay of the land" so to speak when it came to sizing up other would-be gunmen. Without my really knowing it, the name *Cole Stockton* picked up a reputation—gunfighter.

I noticed it one day in a small no-name Texas town near the New Mexico Territory line. I just stepped into a ramshackle saloon and stepped up to the make shift bar, a long wooden plank laid across three fifty-gallon empty beer barrels.

I ordered up a cool beer for myself and as I stood waiting for the lazy bartender to fill the mug, a wild looking youngster of barely eighteen strode smugly into the bar. He stood about five foot six in his stocking feet, but the two Colt revolvers belted around his waist told him that he was ten feet high, and outweighed a bull buffalo.

He acted as loud and boisterous as they come and I noticed that the local patrons sort of grimaced with his arrival. Most avoided eye contact with him. I didn't know him so I paid him no mind. I just stood there hunkered lazily against the bar and waited for that cool beer.

Suddenly, he stood beside me. I looked straight at the back bar, knowing that he wanted me to notice him.

A hissing, sneering voice spoke loudly into my left ear, "You're a stranger here. Most strangers buy me a beer. I'll take one now. My name is *Royce Styles*. Perhaps you have heard of me."

Well, I'd probably heard the same thing from over a dozen others in their small towns, where they bullied most everyone. Something came over me just then, like no other feeling that I'd ever had before.

I turned slightly to face this two gun kid. I looked him straight in the eyes and announced, "I'd be glad to buy you a beer—if you were old enough to drink one—Sonny."

You should have seen the look on his face. He turned beet red and flustered, with surprised embarrassment.

Suddenly, he backed off and with both hands hovering over his Colts, his face turned stern. He challenged, "I am ROYCE STYLES. What name should I put on YOUR tombstone?"

I held my eyes to his and v-e-r-y quietly replied, "Stockton. Cole Stockton."

His hand was in mid-draw when the name suddenly registered. His mouth went slack and his eyes widened. My right hand Colt was already out and leveled straight at his middle. I pulled the trigger.

The reaction from the saloon crowd was one of disbelief. The "kid" that had haunted them with his bullishness now lay dead on the floor.

I holstered my Colt and waited for the local law. Witnesses swore rightly about the circumstances, and the town marshal simply asked me to leave this town. Gladly, I put it miles behind me. I wandered from town to town after that, never staying long anywhere. I would see some country.

CHAPTER TWELVE

Destiny Revealed

A month or so later I found a short-time job as horse wrangler for a small ranch. There were a couple of other young hands working there named Willie and Donovan, and I just naturally fell in with them. They spoke often of their "fast" guns and during lulls in work, they would draw and twirl their revolvers and try to demonstrate fancy tricks with them. I saw no need to match their show.

Periodically, they tried to cajole me into demonstrating my draw. When I declined, they just grinned and made jokes about me, "Guess we'll have to protect Cole when rustlers come upon us." They both laughed out loud, but I paid them no mind. I was confident in my ability.

I thought, at first, that they were a lot of fun. We'd sit around the bunkhouse after supper and play cards, sing a few songs, or just talk of home and family.

On my first payday, after supper, we saddled up and rode as a group into town. We thought that we'd have a few beers at a saloon and maybe dance a bit with some gals employed there. Well, we sipped beer, joked, and danced—we had ourselves a grand ole time.

When it came time to return to the ranch, I learned something more about these boys. They liked to "Yahoo" the town when they left. After we'd mounted and turned to the street, both of them laughed heartily with wild looking eyes. They drew their revolvers as we spurred our mounts down the street, and fired into the air, scaring the daylights out of everyone. They call that—"coming through the rye." I never fired my pistol.

I now had second thoughts about these new found friends, and they weren't exactly good. I let them know that I didn't cotton with that sort of behavior from myself nor from friends, "You boys should not have done that. It gives people poor thoughts about us."

It was Willie that replied, "Aw, Cole. You're just too abiding. Let your hair down and have some fun for crying out loud."Donovan nodded his agreement with Willie.

"Boys," I said with a decidedly sober tone in my voice, "there is fun, but having a laugh with gunplay is not fun. In fact, it's dangerous and downright against my grain. There, I've had my say. You boys should count me out on your games."

From that point on, I threw myself into the work of breaking horses and tried to stay out've their business. Both Willie and Donovan felt my reluctance to continue our friendship and went back to being their own pals.

Soon after, came the day, that I stepped into the bunkhouse and overheard them speaking in low tones about holding up a stagecoach for fun. At least, that was the way that they put it. I made like I hadn't heard a word that they said.

A few days later, the two of them hailed me at the horse corral and asked me to help them round up some strays in the north section. They said that they got the O.K. from Ted, the foreman, for me to help them.

Something didn't set right with me, and I watched their eyes. The thought that I'd overheard their plans and that I wasn't "friendly" to them anymore sort of nagged at the back of my mind. They numbered two, and I was alone. We were quite a ways out from the ranch when they let me know their intentions. I could draw against both of them. They gave me that much.

Willie opened the ball with "Alright, Cole. This is far enough. Get off that horse and face us. We know that you overheard our plans and we don't need anyone telling the law. We know that you won't just ride out and never come back so—we're giving you a chance to face the two of us."

Donovan just grinned and nodded. He was confident that they could take me. Both were confident that they could take me, bury me, and tell the boss that I'd got fed up with the job and just ridden away.

"Don't make me shoot you," I countered.

Disbelieving, both grinned from ear to ear and stepped apart. They looked at me and laughed. They laughed a nervous laugh—their eyes sparkled for just a split second, and then, they both dragged iron.

Wild Bill's lessons, now second nature to me, surged through my mind as my own hand streaked to the grip of my Colt .44. I set myself to take lead.

Willie's first shot zipped through my left sleeve, and I shot him straight in the middle. I then turned the revolver to Donovan.

His pistol belched fire, smoke and hot lead, and I took his shot in the side. He stared at me with widened eyes. He couldn't believe that I just gritted my teeth and grunted loudly.

I turned half way toward him, took careful aim, and shot him dead. He slammed backward in death with a bullet between the eyes.

Even on the ground, Willie still raised his pistol toward me, I shot him again, and he rolled over in death.

I walked up to them and sat down between their bodies. I asked their lifeless forms—neither of whom could hear me, "Why did you make me kill you?"

I sat like that, between them, for a long time. Finally, several hours later, I carried them both back to town and explained the situation to Sheriff Miller. He understood completely, and asked me to leave town, very carefully. I understood.

I decided right then and there, that I had to become a loner. I would ride the trails, from town to town, and try to do things to help people—maybe even to the point of selling my gun.

It seemed then that the name *Cole Stockton* wouldn't let me get a normal job like others. The only fame associated with it, was "hell on wheels—with a six-gun."

I became a lonely man who rode lonely trails. Only in myself did I trust. Another year went by. I visited towns only when I had to. Mostly, I kept to myself and obtained a meal or two by shooting wolves, or chopping wood and mending fences. I grew hard in muscle although still of slender build.

Hard feelings came to me while in the wilds of the Indian Territory. I happened upon a lonely homestead that had been ransacked by ruthless scavengers. The bodies of a young man, a young woman, and barely a-year-old girl child lay just inside the house.

The man had been tied and beaten hard. His eyes bulged in death. His child had been brained with an axe. His wife—well, she had been violated by what seemed to be several men. She seemed to have suffered violently at their hands before they killed her.

I surmised that this simple farmer had been witness to the violation of his wife and subsequent murder. His wrists and neck showed deep rope burns where he was tied. That told me that he had watched all of it until they put a bullet in his brain and rode off with their spoils.

I buried the family and spent the night in their cabin. As I lay in their bed, I found that I could not sleep. I tossed and turned until almost the early hours of the morning. When finally sleep came to me, I dreamed. I dreamed of death and the fiery depths of Hell itself. Within that troubled sleep, I felt a stirring within myself, a chillingly cold hatred of men who would savagely ravage and murder slowly took root within my being.

I didn't know what it meant then, but over the years a story would be told. It would be said of me that when I faced a man over a gun, just before I fired, that he saw the flames of Hell burning within my eyes. I dismissed that story. No man alive could send that fury and fear into the heart and soul of another.

I left that homestead the next morning and traveled south. A week or so later, I rode into Fort Griffin, Texas where after a few days, I got hired on with a cattle drive headed to Abilene, Kansas. It seems that this fella, Nathan Johnston, a local rancher wanted to hire drovers with gun savy because he anticipated trouble with border rustler gangs that rode the Oklahoma-Kansas border. He needed to get all cattle possible to the railhead.

"I need men," he said, "that are steady with gun and horse." I guess that I fit the bill. He ended up hiring three of us to ride with the herd. The other two gents were rough-looking guys, and proclaimed themselves "fast as lightning and twice as mean as a grizzly." They sure liked to let folks know that they were gun-hands. I just sort of stayed to myself, ignoring their attempts at conversation or cards, and rode the point.

Things went fine until we were about five miles inside of the Kansas border. That's when a band of about twenty riders came upon us and I hailed Mr. Johnston. He and about ten of our riders came forward, including the other two hired gunhands. We sat our mounts and waited for the group to state their business.

The group of riders demanded a "passage" tax—well about to the tune of a dollar a head in order to cross *their* land. Naturally, the land was mapped as open domain, free for anyone to cross. The alternative to paying cash money was that they would cut our herd, taking one hundred of the most prized steers for their bounty.

The leader was a hard looking man, about six foot four, who sat a handsome bay horse. He had piercing dark eyes and a sly grin on his face as he explained their intent, "You are crossing my land, your cows are eating my grass and drinking my water. I want restitution. You can pay me one dollar a head and you may continue."

Mr. Johnson looked at him for a long moment before replying, "I understood that this is open range and that I could drive my herd without interference."

The leader replied, "You don't pay, then I'll take some of your steers. I advise you to pay up because you and your drovers don't want trouble from us."

Johnston nodded his understanding, then motioned me forward. "This is my arbitrator. Cole, make him an offer. Bargain with him."

I moved up alongside the leader and looked him straight in the eye. I said softly, "This is free land and we are not paying you. If anything happens, I'm going to shoot you first."

He must've thought himself a fast draw, because he laughed at me, and asked, "Just who do you think you are, kid. I am Todd Albright."

I'd heard the name before. Albright was a notorious gang leader, a killer, and—reputedly extremely vicious in a gunfight.

"The name's Stockton," I said softly, *"Cole Stockton."*

A familiar light shined in his eyes. The same glimmer that I'd seen many times—just before the man grabbed iron and slid that Colt out to line right at me. Suddenly, his hand flashed to his holster, and as his pistol cleared leather, I jumped my horse right at his, drawing my own Colt and firing at the same time.

Since I'd turned his horse sideways, he had to fire across his body, but I was directly in line with him. I thumbed three rounds into his bulk. He jerked sideways in the saddle with each hit, then, fell from his frightened horse to the ground—dead.

That opened the ball, and everyone began firing. I took one that seared across my ribcage, but when it was all over, ten of them rode away, like the Devil was on their heels. Luckily, we lost only two men.

The rest of the way to Abilene went pretty routine, and Mr. Johnston gave me a fifty dollar bonus after the herd was delivered to the stockyard.

As I understood it, Abilene was named after a Bible verse meaning "city of the plains." In any case, it was a wild cow town filled with cattle buyers, drovers, various gunmen, and numerous ladies of the night sometimes referred to as "soiled doves." I decided to get a room at a local hotel, get cleaned up, and see the sights.

After a good soaking in a galvanized bathtub of lukewarm dingy water, I changed into my cleanest clothes and ended up at one of the most popular watering holes in town, and there were quite a few lovely ladies available for dancing, and other things.

One of them, a young dark haired woman, her name was Annie, sort of took a shine to me, and I ended up spending a lot of time in her company that first day in Abilene. We became good friends over several hands of cards, a few beers, and later on, she taught me some dancing steps to keep me from stepping on her toes.

The next day I saw the poster in the general store window.

Shooting Contest

August 9th, 1869 – 2PM at the livery corrals

First Prize - a matched set of Colt Peacemaker revolvers

Entry Fee - $1.00

Well, I had it in mind to win them guns, so I stepped inside the store to register for the contest. Some mighty good shooters entered the contest, including—Bill Hickok, who grinned knowingly when I walked up and laid down my entry fee.

"I think that you will win them." he said to me.

When it was all over and done, I walked away wearing a pair of brand new eagle gripped Colt .44 revolvers. I knew to care for them, and they would serve me well for a long time to come.

I thought about it, and their name seemed right for what I wanted to do with my life—Peacemaker.

CHAPTER THIRTEEN

Rouge's Gallery

Years passed as I drifted from town to town, not staying in one locale too long. I was older now, and still a loner. It wasn't easy to find a job, especially if you were somewhat known by the stories that followed your name. The stories may not have been true—but that didn't matter. The mere mention of your name in some cases prompted decent people to shy away and for "good" lawmen to quietly ask you to leave their towns.

Some men born to the gun simply changed their names and found a niche in some out-and-out corner where they could breathe easier until the inevitable witness recognized them. Then, they would be out riding the grub line again, only to find that selling their *trade* to the highest bidder was the rule of life. Some men died because of it—some got bolder, flaunting their names and reputations to strike fear into the hearts of the common citizen.

On one of those hot and lazy days in the West, I rode slowly into a small New Mexico cattle town. A light breeze warmed my cheeks and periodically a dust devil would suddenly dance before me for several minutes before dispersing in a quick shower to the ground.

I was looking forward to a few days of peace and quiet while deciding where I would travel to next. I'd heard it said by some friends that this town was a haven for a lot of traveling gunmen, and that the law dared not interfere with their stays. It sounded like it would fit the bill for the few days that I had in mind. Word had it, also, that there was a land war brewing between a big cattle rancher in the area and smaller ranchers and farmers. I had recently survived just such a situation in the Indian Territory.

I had been traveling for on to three weeks now, and had not shaved or bathed except for a couple of stints in almost dry creek beds. About the only thing well kept about me was the Colt revolver slung around my slim waist.

I'll admit that folks considered me more than "fairly good" with that six-gun, but I'd not used it for anything against the law. That is not to say that I hadn't dispatched a few unsavory characters with it. I will say that I'd not used it against anyone who didn't deserve killing. My opponents died in a stand up fight—all with the same chance. Because of the circumstances of my fights, there were no "Wanted" posters with the name and description of *Cole Stockton* on them.

Just now, it was all I could do to simply tolerate myself in my clothes damp with sweat. My red-rimmed eyes, from long hours of facing into the sun, wanted undisturbed sleep.

Although the brim of my hat, pulled down for shade, covered most of my face, the dancing and shimmering heat waves of the desert have a way of making a man bone tired, and I felt the way of it. I wanted a long cool drink of water for myself and also my dun horse. A thick beef steak would definitely be a boon to my growling stomach.

I found my way to the local livery to leave my horse for the night, and the hostler looked me over quite suspiciously—like he was trying to place me somewhere in the back of his mind. When strangers appeared, folks just naturally wanted to know who was in town, so they could spread the news to those interested parties watching their back trail.

I had made arrangements for my horse, and with the five dollars left in my pocket, I took my possibles, Winchester rifle, and went looking for a meal, bath, shave, and somewhere to lay my head for the night.

The hostler at the livery recommended a small cantina at the end of the street, and it sounded pretty good to me. He related that a man could get a good meal as well as a cot for the night.

I entered the bat wing doors of the cantina, stepping slightly to the right, letting my eyes become accustomed to the dimly lit room. I slowly took in the clientele, and seeing none that I recognized, shuffled up to the bar. Bar? Hell, it was a long plank laid across three empty fifty-gallon wooden beer barrels. There were makeshift shelves behind the bar, and a heavy set, mustachioed Mexican gent stood at one end, wiping glasses. He eyed me up and down, then lazily walked over to where I stood.

"Senor?" he asked.

"I would like to take a bath, and get something to eat—a room for the night," I told him.

"Si, Senor. One Yankee dollar buys everything for one night—for one dollar more, a girl to warm your heart."

"I'm tired—no girl," I replied, and paid him the dollar.

He led me to a back wash room, where two galvanized tubs sat filled with brackish-looking water. It looked like I wasn't the first customer to use these accommodations that day, but at least, it was a bath. A wall shelf held a few clean towels and I took one.

After setting my saddlebags and bedroll on a homemade, straight backed chair, I unbuckled my gun belt and placed it close to one of the tubs, then shucked my smelly clothes, and eased down into the water. It was only luke warm but it felt good. I just kind of soaked for a while, then took to lathering up with a bar of homemade soap that lay on a small stand next to the tub.

A good hour later, I stepped back into the cantina bar. Fresh clothes, such as they were, felt good after a few weeks of dust and sweat. The bartender had a small table set near the back, next to the kitchen, and he pointed me to it.

I sat down at the table, and a serious young barefooted Mexican girl of about twelve years old brought out a plate of beef and beans and a few tortillas. It wasn't really my thoughts for fine dining, but—the price was right. I washed it down with some cool water that the girl brought to me in a wooden cup from a bucket in the corner.

Now, I was ready for that bed. I felt bone tired from days of horseback riding and wanted nothing more than to drift off, dreaming about fishing in a cool mountain stream.

The bartender showed me to a small room in the back of the cantina that held a narrow cot with tick mattress. Furnishings were sparse. There was one chair next to the cot, and a wooden stand holding a pitcher of water and a wash basin of sorts. A bar of homemade soap lay on top of a neatly folded towel. The single window at the back wall sported a light blue curtain that helped block out the afternoon sun. It would do.

I dismissed the bartender, slipped the door latch, and stowed my gear in a corner. I unbuckled my gun belt and hung it over the back of the chair. My revolver, I laid on the seat, close to hand. Grabbing the thin, gray blanket, I lay back and covered myself. No sooner had my head touched that shabby pillow and I was in dreamland, a large speckled trout on the end of my line.

*   *   *

Morning came, and I decided to grab a bite of a real "Yankee" breakfast. I dressed and slowly sauntered up and down the one dusty main street of this little village. There was one American-run cafe, and I walked over to it.

I entered and sat myself at a back table, close to the wall, then glanced around at those partaking of their morning meal. A few old timers sat near the door sopping up some wheat cakes in molasses or honey and sucking up dark black coffee. It looked good to me, so I ordered up some of the same.

W-e-l-l, I had been there about ten minutes, and was just barely feeling the effects of the coffee when four riders came boiling through town like a whirlwind. They pulled up in front of the cafe, dust flying everywhere. They kept laughing loudly, bullying the café owner, and acting like they owned the town.

I took notice as they entered the door, recognizing every one of them. The list ran like *Rouges Gallery*—Luke Thomas, Ned Short, the infamous Charlie Sturgis, and "Reb" Saunders.

These boys and I had some words a few miles and a few months back up in Oklahoma, on opposite sides of a disagreement, and my side won. They lost some close partners—who weren't so lucky when it came to trading lead with the likes of Cole Stockton.

I wasn't necessarily looking for them, but I was glad to know where they were. At the moment, I definitely hoped that they had awakened in a good mood, as I was looking for a peaceful breakfast.

I leaned back in my chair, right hand sort of lying atop of my holster—just so there would be no mistake of my intentions, should any of them want to try their luck.

Luke Thomas caught my glance first. He stopped in midsentence, and nudged Charlie.

Charlie jerked around, and the look on his face could have churned buttermilk. He looked kind've sick to his stomach.

I just smiled, and said in a rather loud voice, "Hello, boys, here for breakfast? I've already ordered. It'll be a few minutes, though."

Charlie spoke up, "Cole Stockton! I might've known that you'd show up here, with dirt farmers and mustang ranchers needing a gun of their own. This time, it will be different. Just wait and see."

He turned back to his friends, and they took a side table facing the street.

Well, now it was out. If no one in this town knew me by now, they soon would. Besides, Reb Saunders was just itching to try me. He knew it and I knew it.

Reb was a mean one all right, and I had dispatched one of his closest partners during their night raid on a settler's cabin up in Oklahoma. He swore then and there that someone would die for it. Before he could make good on his oath, the whole bunch rode out of town two jumps ahead of a hanging posse, and got lost on the prairie. That was, until now.

I had intended to laze around town and see the sights after breakfast, but under the circumstances, I decided to wait until they rode out of town. I was not in the mood for trouble just yet. I wanted to size up the rest of the town first.

About an hour later, right after those gents walked out the door, mounted their horses and galloped out of town, two of the older men seated near the door as I entered the café stood and walked over to my table.

"Are you really, Cole Stockton? I mean THE Cole Stockton, the gunfighter?" asked one of them.

"Yes, I guess that I am," I replied.

"Mr. Stockton," he began, and I could see it coming. Someone needed help, and I couldn't turn them down, no matter the cost. I had taken a creed unto myself that I would help out those in need. It meant selling my gun, but only to those who needed justice. Most often, there were men enough who sold out to the highest bidder.

"Mr. Stockton, we have need of your services. We saw how you handled those men, and you are not afraid of them. You seem to have knowledge of their methods, and besides—we have read the news accounts of your exploits here and there." He continued, "Those men work for a group that call themselves the *Association*. That is, cattlemen who want nothing more than to run us homesteaders and small ranchers off the range and regain the land for their own cattle. A lot of the available water is on our land, and those ranchers want it. They have been hiring gun-hands right and left for a couple of weeks now, and we have no one except for ourselves. We have asked a few "known" men, and all have refused, saying we can't pay them enough. Will you help us?"

Well, there it was. I was about to jump from the frying pan into the fire again. There was no way that these folks could stand up to the likes of Charlie Sturgis and company. I asked them some pertinent questions, and then agreed to at least meet with them and their group at one of the small farms in the area.

We set the meeting for six o'clock that very evening. They said that they would send riders to all the members of the group to ensure a good attendance. They also assured me that there would be some good ole home cooking available. To tell the truth, I was so tired of eating trail jerky, handouts, and café faire that I would've taken the job just for a few hearty meals.

Anyways, they said that they would do some fancy talking with the rest of their group and see if they could come up with a suitable "fee" for my services. I watched as they filtered out to their mounts and rode out of town.

I signaled the waitress for more of that good black coffee and, after a deep breath, recollected my thoughts.

Some deadly gun play would happen, I had no doubt, and once Reb found out that I had taken up a side, he would come looking for me. He was that way: no playing around, no waiting, just up and take out the competition as fast as possible. Besides, it would serve as fair warning to what the homesteaders would be up against—should they decide to stay and try to defend their land. I would have to watch carefully for him.

The waitress returned with my coffee and a couple of homemade donuts. I momentarily forgot about the situation while I concentrated on devouring those pastries and coffee. Afterward, I walked back down to the cantina and taking a chair out front, sat back against the wall. I wanted to see who else might be in town.

Over the next four hours, I pretty well evaluated the situation by exchanging small talk with the locals who gathered in front of the saloon to whittle, spit, and gossip . For the most part, there were small dirt farmers, small mustang ranchers, and a few larger ranches in the area. The population of the town in general was primarily of Mexican descent, and I saw some fairly pretty young women—all escorted by their parents.

CHAPTER FOURTEEN

Reb's Challenge

At about an hour or so before the meeting time, I went to the livery to saddle up. The hostler gave me another going over, and had this sly grin on his face like maybe it would be my last ride.

I just gave him my own big ole silly grin and swung up into the saddle. "Save my stall," I threw back at him as I turned out into the street.

A good hour's ride following the directions given me by those who approached me in the café brought the old farm house in sight. There were a few wagons and four or five horses tied out front. I dismounted and stepped up to the door. Before I could knock, a right pretty young woman opened it.

She had light brown hair, and hazel eyes. Her deep blue gingham dress matched the blue of her eyes. I never did learn too much about women's wear, or the cloth that they were made of, but I appreciated how that dress seemed to make her eyes even prettier.

She looked straight into my eyes, smiled, and introduced herself. "Mr. Stockton, I am Tara—Tara Schaffer. Welcome to our home." She then turned to the group and announced, "Mr. Stockton's here."

I stepped into the large living room, removing my hat as I did so. The men that I met at the café stood up, as well as about a dozen others.

One by one, they introduced themselves. One young man, Clint Burrow, in about his early twenties, sort of reminded me of myself a few years back. He looked recklessly "devil may care," and wore his gun belt low to his wrist. He was a novice fancying himself as a fast gun, I assumed.

Anyway, he especially took note of how my belt was slung. I had the reputation, and I could read the envy in his eyes. He looked me up and down, and with a slight scowl turned to another gent beside him, saying in low tones, "He don't look like much to me. I'd always pictured the famous Cole Stockton to be much bigger, and more stern looking."

He was surprised and embarrassed when I looked him straight in the eyes and stated, "It ain't how you look, but rather how you stand up to the situation. Right now, I feel like an old man."

I caught the slight smile from Tara, and from a few of the others as well. Another young man, a small rancher's hand—a young cowboy, if you will, stepped forward and extended his hand to me. "Welcome, Mr. Stockton. I am Sandy McGinnis. We need all the help we can get. I am somewhat familiar with hand guns, but not of the skill needed. You can count on my help, though."

Tara was all eyes and ears at Sandy's words, and I knew right away that they had something special between them.

The rest of the folks seemed right nice. We talked about the happenings up to this point. Josh Morgan told of his fences being pulled down and cattle feeding on his small crops. Another man, Seth Watson, told of warnings to get out of the country painted on his stable. There were others who had somewhat the same stories. I listened intently to each as they went around the room, and then, I told them to expect more of the same within the next week. I also told them that very soon, violence would come in the form of night riders who burned property and shot folks who tried to stop them.

One gray haired, slightly robust, crusty old lady wearing overalls, Mary Pickins, stood up and adamantly stated her position on the matter, "I've lived here in this area for nigh on to forty years, and no one is going to run me off my land. Walter, my husband of thirty years, is buried on it, and someday I will lay next to him—but not by the hand of that hired gun scum. They come to my place and I'll shoot them down like me and Walter shot them Apaches and other raiders."

I had to respect her thoughts and her fortitude.

We talked some more, and I gave them all the signs to look for. I advised them each to plan a route from their homes to a place of safety, and to always travel in groups whenever they came to town. I also advised them to have water, ammunition, and food stored in their homes sufficient to withstand a short siege.

I outlined my plan to help them. I would watch the town by day and travel around by night—watching out for the opposition. If anyone heard any rumors of a night raid, or anything else of possible hazard, they should notify me immediately.

The business taken care of, our attention was turned to the kitchen, where the aromas of fried chicken, cobbed corn, and biscuits hung heavy in the air. False apple pie, blueberry pie, or some bread pudding with a berry sauce could finish off the meal, not to mention the one thing I dearly loved—fresh hot black coffee.

I casually reminded those folks of my fee, and they replied with, "Fifty dollars a month, and all the vittles you can eat is what we can pay." A smile spread across my face because these farmers had smartly introduced me to great home-style food before mentioning money.

"You got yourselves some help," I eagerly tossed back, and commenced to dig into that chicken.

Sandy McGinnis and Tara sat next to me. During the dinner and conversation, I sort of took to them. The other young man, Clint, stayed in the background and scowled. It seemed obvious that Clint wanted the affections of this young lady for himself, and Sandy interfered. I would have to watch that situation as it might become kind of sticky.

I stayed until just after ten o'clock, then bid everyone a good evening. It was time to get my plan into action. I figured that Charlie Sturgis and the boys would advise their bosses of my presence and plan for some quick action on their part. I wasn't too far off.

Arriving back in town, I rode up to the livery, dismounted, and led into the stables. The sour-faced hostler was nowhere to be found.

I decided to stable the dun on my own, and when I moved out of the stall, there was Reb Saunders standing in the doorway. He had been eagerly waiting my return, and by the crooked grin on his face, he was fairly sure of himself. "Been waiting fer ya," he drawled. "We got something to settle, and I wanted to be the first and last to bid you a quick journey to Hell."

I was standing back towards the shadows in the stall area, and Reb stood just to the side of the lantern that lit the livery. He had closed the doors. I watched him carefully.

Reb's lower lip twitched slightly, and then, his hand swept toward his pistol.

My right hand was already moving and as he cleared leather, I could see the surprise in his eyes as fire belched from the muzzle of my Colt. The lead took him straight in the chest, and he slammed back against the door.

His Colt fired then; the lead zipped past me to smack into the back of the livery, splintering the wooden planks . I fired again.

The second shot took him close to the first. He jerked hard back against the door again, and I watched his eyes turn upward and glaze over as he slid to the hard dirt floor, the dark stain of blood spreading over his shirt front.

The momentary deafening silence was followed by a scuffling sound and shouts as the door to the livery swung wide open.

The hostler, along with the local law, Marshal Jake Reed, an elderly, overweight, and tired looking man in sloppy dress, entered the livery and looked down upon Reb's lifeless form.

That hostler looked at me with widened eyes, and I could see by his expression that he had expected to find me lying on the floor instead of Reb.

Marshal Reed just looked at me, and shook his head, "I'd call it suicide," he muttered. Then he turned to the hostler, "Jambo, help me carry this body over to Doc Morgan's office. I'll wake him up and make the arrangements."

"No, don't do that," I said. "Send a message to Charlie Sturgis. Tell him that Reb failed to deliver and that Cole Stockton says to come and bury him themselves. They'll come."

While Marshal Reed, Jambo, and the now gathering crowd looked on, I walked up to Reb and punched out two empty brass casings over his body and reloaded. Then I walked out into the night air. It would be morning before anything else happened. This shindig was underway and they would know now that I was ready for them.

*   *   *

Charlie Sturgis stood on the porch of the ranch house watching the growing speck in the distance. Reb was overdue back at the ranch, and that bothered him. He had told Reb, "Be careful—Stockton is not one to fool around with. Just do the job and do it right, don't give him an edge."

The speck grew larger now, and Charlie could clearly make out the rider. It was Jambo, the hostler from the livery. The Rancher's Association paid Jambo good money to provide news about happenings in town, and he aptly delivered. Jambo pulled his roan horse up short in front of Charlie and stared sullenly at him for a long moment.

Charlie looked up at him and asked, "Where is Reb?"

"Reb ain't no more. He got himself kilt. That Stockton feller says for ya'll to come and bury him. He said that you'd understand."

"Yah, I understand. How many shots did Reb get off?"

"Only one. There was two bullets in him—and spaced quite close together."

"Damn. I guess it is going to take more than one man to take Stockton out of this play. I will have to think on this a while."

CHAPTER FIFTEEN

Night Riders

It was nigh about three o'clock that afternoon when the ranch wagon and five riders slowly rumbled up to Doc Morgan's office.

I sat my chair in front of the cantina and watched as Charlie Sturgis, Ned Short, Luke Thomas, and two other rough looking gents entered the Doc's combination office and funeral parlor. They exited a few minutes later with Reb's blanket-covered body.

I stood up and walked to the end of the cantina front. Charlie Sturgis looked straight at me, and I could tell what was going through his mind: He was a wondering if he should start a play and carry this thing further. Well, here I was, ready and waiting on him to make a move. He didn't like it, and decided to wait.

The look in his eyes told a cold story. He dearly wanted to touch that revolver at his belt, but good sense kept him from doing it. Charlie liked an edge, and right now, I had the advantage because I was ready for him. He knew what I could and would do.

Charlie also knew that even with four other men, he would be the first to go, and that fact didn't set well with him. No. He would wait for a time when I wasn't set and waiting.

I watched closely as they loaded Reb's body up and rumbled out of town toward the cattle range.

I realized that they were quite worked up now, and tonight they would be wanting revenge. I thought about all those farmer people. Who would be most likely to get hit tonight? They would start with those least able to defend themselves. That was their pattern, the route of cowards.

I thought about that sweet old lady, Mary Pickins, and knew that I'd best ride on over there and have some supper with her.

An hour later found me at the Pickins' spread. A broad smile spread across her face as I rode up to her door and slid out of the saddle. The smile, however, turned to a serious look as I reached up, took saddle bags and slid my Winchester from the scabbard before stepping up to the door.

Mary cocked her head slightly, and with questioning eyes, looked thoughtfully at me. Her previous smile turned into a determined set jaw expression as she asked, "They coming here tonight Cole?"

"I think so," I replied. "I think that they will start right here."

"Then, we'll be ready for them," she said, matter of factly, and turned to take up a long double-barreled shotgun from behind the door. I followed her into the house and when I stepped inside, my nose told me that she had been baking bread all day, and had just put a pot of coffee on the stove.

Mrs. Pickins got out a couple of boxes of shells from a desk drawer and looked to make sure the boxes were full. She put them on the table next to the kitchen window. I set my Winchester and extra ammunition next to the table as well and went to stable my horse in the tool shed next to the house.

When I returned, we sat down at her kitchen table, and Mary cut into one of those loaves of bread. Fresh churned butter and honey sat on the table and she motioned me to help myself. She didn't have to ask a second time. I dearly love fresh bread and honey, Hers tasted delicious.

Mary and I sat there watching the rays of the sun slowly fade over the land. No lamps would be lit tonight. I wanted to keep them boys guessing as to whether or not anyone was up and about.

Our eyes grew accustomed to the darkness, as we sat there watching out the windows. The moon was only slight, but we could make out natural shadows along the fencing, tool shed, and barn.

Around midnight I saw the first slightest movement along the corral. "Here they are," I said softly to Mrs. Pickins. "Get ready, because we are going to open the ball."

I lined up my Winchester on one of the dark shadows and squeezed off. A scream of pain shrieked from the shadow, and then bright orange stabs of flame erupted all around the house. Molten lead smacked into the door, the window sills, through the windows, and into the walls.

"There must be at least a dozen," I thought aloud, and then continued with, "minus one."

"Make that two," shouted Mary, as she squeezed off her shotgun. The boom was deafening. I kept up a steady fire with my Winchester, sending hot lead to every muzzle flash that I saw.

In a matter of minutes, the quick flame of a match, and then a fiery brand arched into the air and landed just inside Mary's small barn to set it blazing good. That hay-strewn barn went up like the fires of Hades itself, and the entire ranch yard lit up. Those boys sure messed up. All that light from the burning barn gave us the targets that we wanted, and from there, we picked them off more easily.

Five men were down, and the rest scrambled for their mounts and took off. We ran out the door toward the burning barn.

Mary had little stock in the barn, and what was there had escaped the fire by kicking out walls and taking off in multiple directions. I would track them down in the morning.

We checked the five fallen men and, unfortunately for them, our shots were true. All lay dead. Ned Short sprawled grotesquely and bloody. He had taken a full shotgun blast in the mid section. Two of the Rouges Gallery were now gone. Things were going to get hot now.

There was nothing the two of us could do about the barn. We stood helplessly watching it collapse into a fiery pile. Mary Pickins turned to me and said, "A small price to pay for what might have been. If not for you, they could have come in here and burned everything—even killed me. I hate to say it, but I couldn't have fought them by myself, Cole. Come, I'll help you bury them."

"No," I said, "we won't bury them here. We'll put them in the back of your wagon. I'll take them to town. I want the whole town to know what kind of men these are: men who would raid an elderly woman's home, and try to burn her out."

"That sure won't set right with folks around here," she replied.

"I'm counting on it. We need all the help we can get. If we can show those townspeople just what these boys are like, they might just help us by passing information along whenever they hear something."

We went back into the house and Mrs. Pickins fired up that wood burning stove and made some fresh coffee. Morning came, and she filled me up with thick sliced bacon, a stack of wheat cakes, and about four eggs, over easy.

"A growing boy like you has got to eat," she laughed, while setting that plate in front of me. I ate heartily.

I had barely finished breakfast when riders came galloping into her farm yard. A quick glance out of the window showed our company to be friendly.

Sandy McGinnis and Tara Schaffer dismounted, taking in the scene of burned barn and dead raiders, and stepped to the door. "Come on in and join us for some breakfast," called Mrs. Pickins aloud. "There's plenty for all."

We talked over Mary's cooking, and I explained the night's activities. Sandy and Tara volunteered to track down the frightened stock and return them. I would take the dead into town. I wanted to see the faces of the townspeople, and especially Jambo's face.

*   *   *

It was around noon when I drove Mary's wagon into town and right up to the front of Marshal Reed's office. Townspeople gathered around as I hauled the bodies out of the wagon, and lined them up on the boardwalk in front of the jailhouse door.

I turned to face the ever growing crowd of on-lookers. "This here is what happens to evil men who would attack a lonely widow's home in the middle of the night," I stated loud enough for all to hear.

I continued, "These men belong to the Cattlemen's Range Association, and they can bury them. Take this as fair warning. This will be the fate of any who ride, burn, and kill in the night. I don't know what the Association pays, but it ain't going to be worth it. My name is Cole Stockton, and from this day forth, I will track down and shoot any man identified as raiding farms and homes in the name of the Association."

CHAPTER SIXTEEN

Ambushed

Clint Burrow was riding herd on a dozen rangy steers on his small mustang ranch when the five riders came out of the trees. He pulled up sharp and scrutinized the men. They all appeared to be rough, hard men, and all wore gunbelts like they knew how to use them. Clint recognized the leader as they got closer.

Charlie Sturgis led the low life marauders. The five as one drew their weapons, and Clint hesitated only a moment before jerking his buckskin around hard and spurring him into a dead run towards his house. The five men also spurred their mounts.

Molten lead whistled past Clint's head and body. He drew his revolver, and turned to fire back at his pursuers. Suddenly, the buckskin horse screamed and fell headlong to the ground—dead.

Clint was thrown clear of the stumbling horse, but lay stunned as the riders galloped up to surround him. Charlie Sturgis grinned from ear to ear. "Say boys," he chuckled, "this here's that wild mustanger ranch kid who thinks he's fast with a gun. I think I'll give him the chance to prove it."

Charlie handed his reins to one of his men and dismounted. He strode up to Clint and looked him straight in the eyes. Clint Burrow felt the icy cold stare reflective of a dozen souls of those that Sturgis had murdered. He felt uneasy and his very soul trembled with fear.

One of Sturgis's men dismounted and picked up the kid's gun. He walked up to him and dropped it into the kid's holster, then backed away, grinning.

Charlie Sturgis stepped back five paces, always looking Clint straight in the eyes. "On the count of three, kid. Townsend, count to three."

"One!" Clint Burrow was sweating.

"Two!" Those eyes—piercing—staring right through him. Charlie looked like Satan himself to Clint.

"Three!"

Clint Burrow's hand was reaching for his gun butt as he saw Charlie Sturgis flash his right hand to his belt. Clint's hand gripped the butt; the weapon was rising from his holster. It was the fastest he had ever moved, but as his pistol cleared the holster, he looked with horror at Charlie's Colt. The deadly bore was staring right at him. Charlie had the hammer thumbed back and he was squeezing the trigger.

Fire belched from Charlie's pistol and the molten lead caught Clint straight in the chest. He grunted as it slammed him backward. His eyes blurred and his finger tightened around the trigger of his own weapon, discharging it into the ground. Clint Burrow saw his life pass before him as Charlie walked up to him and calmly said "Goodbye, kid." Charlie Sturgis shot Clint between the eyes.

"Leave him here," Sturgis groaned as he waved away a couple of his men who approached to dispose of the body. "Someone will find him and bury him. It will be a warning to all those small ranchers and homesteaders that we mean business."

Charlie Sturgis remounted and all five men rode off slowly, never looking back.

*   *   *

Sandy McGinnis and Tara Schaffer heard the crackling of gunfire in the distance. They turned their mounts toward the direction of the gunfire and heeled them into a gallop. A long silence ensued. They slowed their mounts to a walk and strained their ears, listening for more sounds. Suddenly, two more quick cracks split the air, and they rode hard in that direction.

"It's coming from just over that next ridge!" shouted Sandy to Tara. "It's at Clint Burrow's place!"

Sandy was in the lead as they leaned forward against their horses' necks, working their way up the steep grade toward the top of the ridge. Sandy reached back and pulled his Henry repeating rifle from the scabbard as he neared the top. Tara did likewise and pulled her saddle carbine from her scabbard. They reached the crest of the ridge in time to watch as Charlie Sturgis ended young Clint's life.

"Oh, no!" cried Tara. "I think that they've just killed Clint."

Tears streamed from her eyes as she moved to spur her mount toward the grisly scene. Sandy quickly grabbed her reins and stubbornly held on tight. "There's nothing we can do right now. We'll go down there and take care of him when they've gone. Do as I say, or we'll be lying there beside him, or worse."

Tara knew that Sandy was right. Those men were hardened, cold, vicious killers and it would take someone equally as hard to deal with them—someone like Cole Stockton.

They watched as the five men rode off, and then slowly made their way down to the scene.

*   *   *

Two hours later I drove Mary's wagon back into her ranch yard. Sandy McGinnis and Tara Schaffer stood alongside Mary. Their somber looks told me that something was amiss.

"They killed Clint," sobbed Tara with newly misting eyes.

"We saw it from a distant ridge," said Sandy. "It was Charlie Sturgis. I saw him walk up to a downed Clint and shoot him dead. We took Clint home to his folk's place. They were heartbroken. Cole, Clint was wild and crazy, but he didn't deserve to die like that. Why didn't they just leave him there wounded?"

I took a long moment before looking at them, replying, "Charlie felt that he had to kill him," I said quietly. "First, a wounded man is likely to heal and then track you down, and kill you. Second, Charlie wanted to leave a message to all you folks. He intends to do the same with anyone who opposes him. His message is clear. Sell out, get out, or die."

I knew then that it was time to make it personal between me and Charlie, and I saddled up my dun. I had just put boot to stirrup, and was swinging up into the saddle when Sandy stepped out of the house and looked up at me.

"You're going after Charlie, aren't you?"

"No, Sandy, I'm going to send Charlie Sturgis a message. He will come to me, and we will end this thing."

I turned the dun to leave, then, suddenly drew rein, and looked back toward him. "You take care of these fine women. I'll be back tomorrow."

Dusk found me dismounting in front of the livery. Jambo, the hostler, was there with his usual sour face. He sort of stared at me when I dismounted and led the dun to the rearmost empty stall. As I passed him, I detected a hint of nervousness in his manner. A closer look at him caught the bulge of a sidearm in the hostler's waistband and something registered in the back of my mind. Jambo had not carried iron before, and I grew wary, keeping the dun between him and me.

Once I had the dun in the stall, I slid that Winchester out of the scabbard, and with the unmistakable, slightly audible metallic click near the door of the stable, I jacked a round into the chamber.

Jambo's first shot smacked through the boards of the stall, barely missing the dun who kicked and reared. I dashed across the open space to the opposite stall, and hot lead smacked a trail behind me.

I rolled to the dirt floor, and crawled up to the entrance. He had fired about four rounds now and should have only two bullets left. I peered through the slats of the stalls and caught his outline. He was hunkered down with that revolver ready.

"Let's see what a .44-40 can do to those slats," I thought, sliding the barrel of my Winchester through the spacing. I squeezed off.

I didn't kill him, but I sure burned his hide good. That rifle lead smashed through the wood plank and threw splinters everywhere.

He screamed out in surprise and pain, and I stepped out into the open area, Winchester in hand. Jambo still held that pistol in one hand and was trying to pull a burr of splinters from his backside with the other.

I called for him to drop the gun. "Jambo! Drop that pistol or your next move is your last!" He looked wild-eyed at me for only a second, then defiantly leveled that pistol at me. I shot him dead.

I stepped over his body and started out of the livery doors when lead whistled past me and smacked into the livery walls. The crackling of pistol and rifle shots split the air, and I hit the dirt again, rolling to the right. Dirt furrows pillowed up all around me as molten lead plowed into the hard earth of the street.

I couldn't see them yet, but there were at least three guns firing at me from the shadows. I lined up on one darkened alleyway and fired. A surprised yell rewarded my effort. I had hit someone.

I rolled quickly to the left, and fired at another stab of orange flame. This time there was a choked scream, before I saw the shadow stumble into the street holding his chest. He fired at me again and his next round burned along my shoulder as I remembered Bill Hickok's philosophy, "Take careful aim and shoot the man dead."

I concentrated on the man's middle, set my jaw, and squeezed off. That slug jerked him to his toes and slammed him back on the road. The firing stopped and I guessed that the last man had fled the scene.

I cautiously walked up to the fallen ambusher. It was Luke Thomas, still barely alive. I looked down on him and he tried to speak. Bright red blood oozed from his mouth and seeped something fierce from his chest. I knew that I'd hit him in the lungs. He gasped out the words, "You're a hard man to kill, Stockton. I didn't want it this way, but Charlie," Luke fought to catch his breath, "Charlie said it was the only way."

I watched Luke's eyes slowly glaze over and then his body relaxed to lay still. He had taken his final breath.

Three of the Rouges Gallery had perished, and now it was definitely personal between me and Charlie.

Townspeople slowly and warily appeared on the street to look over the bodies. Tired old Marshal Reed shuffled his way across the street to an alleyway, taking stock of the body lying there. I watched as he knelt down for a moment, then, stood up and shook his head from side to side indicating that the ambusher was dead. He then walked up next to me and looked down on the lifeless body of Luke Thomas.

"You can make the arrangements on Jambo and these two men, Marshal. The next one has already dug his own grave."

I turned and went back to the livery. The dun must've figured that we'd be traveling again because he definitely wanted out of that stall. I didn't blame him one bit. I had been the target of several bullets in that building and the cool, clean evening air would feel mighty good.

The dun moved quickly, fidgeting nervously about, stepping here and there as I spoke softly to him and gained control of the reins. I got him settled down and once again swung up into the saddle. Leaning down as we cleared the livery doors, we moved out into the dusty street and then trotted through town with a purpose. Folks watched as I rode steadily past them, and you could see the speculation in their eyes. I thought that I heard one old timer remark, "There goes death on a dark horse".

CHAPTER SEVENTEEN

Quest for Justice

Early dawn found me on the ranch that hired Charlie and gang. I boldly rode up to three cowhands hunkered down around a campfire having breakfast. The three of them stood up as I approached, none of them looked to be gunmen. I asked them point blank, "Where can I find Charlie Sturgis? I have business with him." They could see by my determined face that I was not in a friendly mood.

One man nodded his understanding, "You're Cole Stockton. I seen you in town." He pointed off toward the north, "Sturgis and his boys use a line shack about two miles that way. You'll come to a creek. The cabin is back in the trees."

I thanked him for the information and, touching spur to the dun, loped off in that direction. A short time later, I crossed the creek, dismounted, and worked my way on foot to one side of the cabin. I called out for Charlie to step out and face me. There was no reply, so I cautiously worked my way to the door and flung it open. I stepped inside the cabin, revolver at the ready, expecting to be met with flame and hot lead. I encountered only silence.

The place was deserted. I quickly surveyed the room. By the looks of it, Charlie had packed his duff in a hurry and was on the run. This time, however, I was going to track him down and see to it that no one ever suffered by his gun again.

I needed supplies and a few dollars to keep me in vittles so I swung by the Schaffer place. Sandy and Tara were there. Mr. Schaffer listened intently while I related the latest details about Charlie and company. "The worst is over," I told them, "Sturgis is running and I'm going after him. Without Charlie, the others have lost the inclination for violence. You and your friends should continue to stick together. You must petition the governor for able bodied, honest law in your town."

John Schaffer went to his desk to give me the "wages," when I told him that the trouble was over.

Sandy walked out to the hitching post with me. As I mounted up, I turned to him with that ole silly grin of mine spreading across my face— I looked down at him and said, "You need to marry that girl."

Before Sandy could reply, I heeled the dun into an easy lope and headed back to pick up Charlie's trail. He was headed toward the wilds of the Colorado Territory.

*   *   *

Three weeks later, I was still following Charlie's trail from town to town. He was moving fast. At the last small semblance of civilization, a one-horse town, the bartender in the single cantina remembered Charlie from two days before.

The man said that Charlie looked quite haggard and uneasy. He went on to relate that he appeared nervous, and kept looking over his shoulder, staring at people. Folks shied away from him.

I thanked him for the information and again trotted off in the direction that Charlie was headed. Evening came. I knew that I soon had to stop and rest. That's when I saw the flicker of a campfire in the distance. I slowed to a walk, and with Winchester at the ready cautiously approached the campsite. Good manners dictated that I hail the campsite and wait for an invitation before entering. But, in this case, I was trailing a killer and I wanted to make sure that I wasn't walking into the wrong camp. I proceeded carefully, and could smell the coffee brewing and the rabbit broiling on the spit before I got within hailing distance of the camp.

I continued slowly toward the camp until I could make out the features of the single inhabitant at this lonely site. It definitely wasn't Charlie Sturgis.

He was an older man in his mid-sixties, I would say, by the grayish hair at his temples and whiskered face. He was tall and lanky. A worn black Stetson sat lazily back on his head and he wore a working ranch hand's outfit of jeans, faded blue shirt, pale suspenders and a red bandana. He wore his gun belt high on his waist and I knew that he was no gunman.

"Hallo the camp!" I audibly spouted out and waited only a long moment before a good natured "Welcome to my camp" bid me to enter.

I slowly took in the camp surroundings. There were about a dozen or so good, solid looking horses lazily grazing around the campsite. I took him for a wild "mustanger," a man who hunts wild horses and wrangles the wild out of them for sale.

I also took in the Henry repeating rifle lying over his saddle and blanket. It was close to hand, but the man never paid serious attention to it. He looked up at me, and I guess I must've looked as hungry as I was, because a big friendly grin spread over his suntanned face, and he said, "Howdy. Strip that gear from your hoss and have some coffee and a bite to eat. Ain't got much, but you are welcome to share."

He didn't have to ask twice. I slid wearily off the dun and stripped my gear, then turned it to graze with the others. I set my gear down across the fire from his and laid my Winchester over the saddle and blankets, just like his.

He watched me carefully and I could see that he was studying on me with a practiced eye. He paid close attention to the way that my Colt was slung low around my waist. He didn't say anything, but he took it all in.

We ate a leisurely meal and that coffee was some of the best that I had ever tasted, strong and black. We talked some while we ate, and I began to relax. This old man was quite a likeable character.

"Name's Jesse," he commented, "I come out here back in '42 with Fremont and company. Well, I liked what I saw country-wise and decided to stay. There were some hard times, but I weathered each, and now, I've got a nice business in finding and breaking wild horses."

That comment struck a note, thinking momentarily back to Jasper Rollins and me doing some horse hunting of our own. I reckoned that ole Jesse and I had something in common and replied back as such,

"Did some wild horse hunting myself a while back. Made some good money at it too. But, times changed and so did I."

"I know full well what you mean," countered Jesse. "I'd tried my hand at a few things before settling on the horse business. I'd done some freighting along the Oregon Trail, wrangled for the Pony Express, and even tried my hand at prospecting a bit. My travels took me hither and yon, and one day I found this valley in the Colorado Territory, and decided, right then and there, that this was my home."

After we ate our fill, he pulled out the makings and rolled us each a smoke. He handed me one, then reached into the fire and we lit up with a burning brand. Then, we just laid back on our bedrolls, leisurely smoked those "homemades" and Jesse continued to talk. Myself, I was content to listen. You could learn a lot about a man just by listening to his experiences and about his travels.

Jesse told stories of hunting wild horses, and of fighting off wild Indians and rustlers. He talked quite a bit about a young niece that he had down in Texas. He said that she was quite a horsewoman, or at least, would be one day. He went on to say that he hoped that she would visit his ranch someday. I could easily tell that he held a deep affection for her.

It must've been midnight when we said our goodnights and settled down for the night. I slept with my Colt close to hand, for a man of my reputation could not be too trusting, even with a seemingly honest man. There were other dangers that could unexpectedly present themselves. I felt that Jesse did likewise.

The early light of dawn brought me out of my short pleasure and back to the grim business at hand. I saddled up the dun while the old man brewed us up another pot of that good coffee and cooked a quick breakfast; some of the best biscuits and bacon I had ever tasted. The time came, and before I swung up into the saddle, the old man looked carefully at me and said, "Son, I like your makings. Don't suppose that you are a hunting a job? My horse ranch is up over the passes into the Lower Colorado. I will be returning there after delivering this bunch, and I have need of a couple more hands."

"At the moment, I'm following a friend," I replied, "Perhaps at some later time, when I'm finished with my business." He nodded his head, knowing full well what I meant.

"Any time, Son. Just ride up over the passes into the wilds and the first town you come to, ask for ole Jesse Sumner."

I waved to him as I rode out, and he waved back, "Take care, Son. May the Almighty ride with you."

*   *   *

Charlie Sturgis was running scared for the first time in his life. As the third man in the shadows who had missed Cole Stockton with four shots, that was an omen to him.

Jambo, the hostler, was dead. Mike Canton had slumped lifelessly in the adjoining alley with Stockton's first bullet in him. He had watched breathlessly as Luke Thomas fired at Stockton from across the street, the bright orange flame of his Colt spitting lead that only furrowed up alongside of Stockton's prone figure.

He saw Stockton take careful aim at the flash of Luke's revolver and then fire. He watched unbelieving as Luke screamed a choked cry of anquish when the ugly thunk hit him in the chest.

Charlie watched as Luke staggered out of his hiding place in the darkened alley and tried to level his pistol at Stockton again. He watched, frozen in his tracks, as Stockton lined up and carefully squeezed off, hitting Luke Thomas again in the chest, jerking him up and slamming him down.

At that split second, Charlie Sturgis envisioned his own dead body lying sprawled in the dusty street and lost his nerve. He turned and ran to the back of the alley. Grabbing his wild-eyed brown horse, he scrambled up into the saddle, spurred its flanks and galloped wildly out of town.

Charlie had to escape the nagging vision in his brain that his time on earth was limited. He had to put as much distance between himself and Cole Stockton as he could, and to keep that distance. The four of them had tried to sneak shoot Cole Stockton and failed. The word would be out. Stockton would come for him, and Charlie Sturgis would be no more. Charlie now knew that he, himself was a walking dead man.

Charlie rode aimlessly through the night, and as the days passed, from town to town, spending no more than a few hours in each. The nagging vision of Cole Stockton coming quietly up behind him ate away at the edges of his sanity until, finally, his eyes were cold and lifeless. There was no real life within his body. If a man could look deep into the mirror of Charlie's soul, he could see an anguished figure already burning in the brimstone fires of Hell.

CHAPTER EIGHTEEN

Judgment Day

I followed Charlie Sturgis's trail for four months, and finally, as luck would have it, lost him. Word was out that he'd left the Territory and gone to California. Another rumor had it that he shucked his guns and lit out for back East. Yet, another rumor repeated frequently was that he went to Mexico and was killed by a gang of desperadoes. The most improbable one I heard was that he turned into the desert and was probably killed by marauding Apaches.

Six months later, a good source informed me that Charlie was in Santa Fe with some new partners and that he had killed a young cowboy over a saloon girl. The source said he was faster than ever, and extremely vicious. Charlie had turned into the worst of men. I decided to ride towards Santa Fe and check out this story as I still owed Charlie.

I now rode a handsome roan that I'd traded my dun for, down south. I named him Chino.

Enroute to Santa Fe, I stopped in at Las Vegas, New Mexico Territory for a noon meal. I had finished my meal at the small cafe and begun walking down the dirt street when two ugly mean gents staggered out of the Ace of Spades Saloon.

One of them grabbed a young townswoman passing by, and tried to force his attentions on her. She screamed for assistance as the biggest of the two pawed at her dress.

I don't cotton much to that kind of behavior, and interfered, "Unhand that woman and let her be!"

"You mind your own business, mister," one snarled back at me. I took another step forward and as I did, the big one holding her glared at me with, "You were told to mind your own business, you do it!"

I fairly leaped straight up on the boardwalk and forcibly pushed one back, but he quickly recovered and set himself in the gunman's stance. Suddenly, the second one roughly pushed the frightened woman away, snarled obscenities at me and dragged iron. Five seconds later they were both dead.

The woman lay on the ground, disheveled and sobbing. I moved to her and helped her up. She leaned against me trembling as townspeople gathered around us. Within minutes, the sheriff arrived on the scene and immediately recognized me as Cole Stockton. I could see in his eyes that he had no love for known gunmen in his town. Witnesses advised him of the situation, and I was free to leave at his kind request.

I got Chino from the livery and rode out of town just as the afternoon Butterfield coach was coming in.

Funny thing about that stage, it was as if there was something pulling at me from that coach. I couldn't put my finger on it, but I suddenly felt more lonely than ever. Well, I had a chore to do, and it wasn't getting done by worrying about a simple stagecoach. I turned toward the West and put it out of my mind.

*   *   *

I hit into Santa Fe to find out that Charlie Sturgis had departed some weeks earlier. A saloon keeper had overheard parts of the conversation between Charlie and his current riding partners indicating that they were headed toward El Paso. He also appraised me of the swift and deadly gunfight between Charlie and that young cowboy. It seems that Charlie was indeed alive and meaner than ever.

"One other thing," the saloon keeper said to me, "it was like he didn't care."

"What do you mean?" I asked.

"It was like Sturgis didn't care if he got shot himself or not. He just stood there, drew his Colt and shot that boy down. Shot him three times. The last one to make sure he was dead. Then he turned and finished his beer. Before he left, I looked into his eyes, and there was no God-fearing life in them. Not a glimmer."

I thanked the bartender for the information, climbed up on Chino and headed toward El Paso, Texas. Something had to be done about Charlie, and I hoped that I could find him before someone else died by his gun.

I found a similar situation in El Paso. Charlie had been there, but had left, presumably on his way to Prescott, Arizona.

Not relenting, I had picked up his trail again, and felt an ever pressing need to follow it.

I followed Charlie all over the Southwest. He moved fast, and the story was always the same. He left a trail of freshly dug graves and grieving families.

Now, three months later, I heard that he was in Las Cruces, New Mexico Territory. I rode hard and fast.

I arrived into Las Cruces late in the evening. The main street felt lively with piano music and boisterous laughing coming from the several saloons along the street front. I pulled Chino up to one of the saloons and dismounted.

"I sure could use a cool beer to cut the dust," I thought.

I stepped up on the boardwalk and entered the bat wing saloon doors. Several cowboys and other men seated at tables around the door looked up at me for a second, and then, the name, *Cole Stockton*, ran around the room amid the din of the crowd. Suddenly, you could have heard a pin drop.

I immediately took in the room at a quick glance.

Charlie Sturgis and two other rough-looking gents were seated at a table in the far corner of the saloon.

All of a sudden, men quickly got up from their tables and moved to the walls. There was nothing but space between me and Charlie and those other two outlaws.

All three just sat there looking at me. I didn't know the other two personally, but I knew what kind of men they were. The one with the Mexican outfit on had to be "Sonora" Jim Cattrell, a mean hombre in his own right. The other appeared to "Snake" Wilson, nicknamed so for his beady looking eyes.

I took a quick deep breath and stepped toward them.

Charlie just smiled at me with an evil crooked grin and slipped up from his chair. The other two followed suit. I watched their eyes closely as they spread out a mite.

"You're dead, Charlie," I said. Men nearest the door fled outside for safety. Others dove behind the piano and the bar. A split second later, four men's hands flashed for their weapons, and the crowd along the walls rammed themselves to the floor.

Fire and hot lead belched from revolver muzzles. The acid smell of gunpowder filled the room as molten lead smacked into walls, mirror, bar glasses, tables, and men.

My right hand Colt leaped into my hand and rose fluidly to level at Charlie. I also drew my second Colt from the back of my belt. I squeezed off my first round, taking Charlie in the mid section.

A bullet whizzed past my left ear, and I immediately turned the Colt to Sonora Jim. I snapped a quick one in his direction. He ducked and my bullet smacked into the wall behind him.

My third round thunked hard into Snake Wilson's chest. He was slammed back against the wall to slide down along it to the floor. A bloody streak followed his slide to the floor.

Bullets flew all over the room. I clearly expected to get hit at any time.

Surprisingly, Charlie was still standing there, firing at me. I felt his first bullet whistle through my shirt sleeve. He fired too fast. His second whistled close to my right ear as it flung my Stetson into the air and smashed into the already broken bar back mirror. Glass fragments literally flew across the room.

I again turned my attention to Charlie and shot him once more, close to the first. He jerked back with the impact of the slug, but still managed to stay on his feet. He fired at me a third time and I felt this one burn along my waist. I winced with the sharp pain.

I dropped my left hand revolver and pressed my hand against the wound in an attempt to stop the bleeding.

Sonora was on his hands and knees, crawling along the wall. He overturned a table, crouching behind it. I shot right into it with two rounds in quick succession. Splinters flew everywhere as I heard his body thud back against the wall.

That emptied my revolver. I stood shakily on my feet reloading and looking straight into Charlie's blank and near lifeless eyes.

He hovered there, struggling to raise that Colt again. I methodically ejected three spent cartridges, reloaded three fresh ones and turned the cylinder. I cocked my revolver, pointed it straight at Charlie and waited.

Charlie's Colt was lining up straight at me. I squeezed the trigger.

Charlie jerked with the impact. I fired again, and he stumbled backward against the wall. I fired the third bullet into his chest. Charlie again jerked with the impact, then fell straight forward to lay face down on the plank floor.

The saloon crowd began to peer up from the floor as the silence filled the room. Others from the outside, curious to see the carnage, carefully reentered the saloon.

I stood there bleeding from the wound in my side, reloading my once again empty Colt.

Then, I walked slowly up to Charlie, watching Snake at the same time. Snake lay dead in a slumped grotesque pile. I hooked my boot under Charlie and turned him over. His glazed and lifeless eyes stared up at the ceiling, and I spoke softly to myself, "The last of the Rouges Gallery."

Suddenly, a revolver cracked behind me and I turned, cocking and leveling my own Colt at the same time.

Sonora Jim had struggled to his knees and had tried with his last ounce of life to shoot me in the back. He now lay sprawled lifeless on the floor, his revolver cocked but unfired.

A stocky, dark haired man stood over Sonora Jim's body, a smoking Colt revolver in his right hand. On his vest was pinned a Deputy United States Marshal's badge. He looked at me, and said, "You must be Cole Stockton. I have been trailing you since your shooting scrap in Las Vegas. A Federal Judge wants real bad to talk with you. I was sent to bring you before him with haste, that being over four months ago. You shore move around a lot."

*　　*　　*

Deputy U.S. Marshal Jamison turned the scene in the saloon over to the local sheriff, and accompanied me to the doctor's office where I was patched up. He hadn't asked for my revolvers, so I just naturally kept them. I asked about this judge that wanted to meet me, but he was all mysterious, or truly unknowing about it.

"Marshal Jamison, tell me about this judge. Who is he and what does he want of me?" I pressed for information.

"Stockton, Judge Wilkerson has his reasons. I suspect he'll explain everything when you two meet."

Seeing as I had no other immediate business, other than complete curiosity, I rode up to the Colorado Territorial Seat with Jamison. That's when I was introduced to Judge Joshua Bernard Wilkerson. He stood close to six feet two, had brown hair with a touch of gray, steel gray eyes, and a preacher-like smile. I kind've liked him from the start.

"Mr. Stockton," he began, "I have studied your reputation and followed your path of doings for quite some time now. I cannot allow a man of your obvious reputation, skill and experience to continue gallivanting all over the countryside and shooting people. That is, unless you wear this." He reached into his desk drawer and handed me a Deputy U.S. Marshal's Star.

"Will you accept the job? You will report directly to me. The pay is fifty dollars a month and found, with all the bullets you can shoot. This territory is plagued with all sorts of rascals—scavengers, rustlers, marauders, and other sorts of ill repute. I need a good man to help clean up this territory."

I looked straight into Judge Wilkerson's eyes, and I saw my chance to do something good for folks. Besides, I was a bit tired of selling my gun to outfits. This would be a real job that would allow me to keep my personal oath of using my gun to help folks in need.

I pinned on the badge and raised my right hand. "I, Cole Stockton, do solemnly swear that I will uphold the laws of the Constitution and to protect—so help me God."